"I don't know why you're being so unfriendly.

"If it's money, I fully intend to pay you for all the trouble you've gone to," Sheila snapped.

Anger rose swiftly from somewhere within him. "Don't start throwing your money at me. I don't need it, and I sure don't want it. Not Danforth money."

"What's wrong with Danforth money?" Sheila demanded.

Mike was silent for a minute. "Maybe you didn't catch my name. I'm Mike *Barlow*."

"So?"

"So this is the longest time anyone from my family and anyone from yours has had anything to do with the other in ninety years."

Dear Reader,

Spellbinders! That's what we're striving for. The editors at Silhouette are determined to capture your imagination and win your heart with every single book we publish. Each month, six Special Editions are chosen with *you* in mind.

Our authors are our inspiration. Writers such as Nora Roberts, Tracy Sinclair, Kathleen Eagle, Carole Halston and Linda Howard—to name but a few—are masters at creating endearing characters and heartrending love stories. Their characters are everyday people—just like you and me—whose lives have been touched by love, whose dreams and desires suddenly come true!

So find a cozy, quiet place to read, and create your own special moment with a Silhouette Special Edition.

Sincerely,

The Editors
SILHOUETTE BOOKS

LYNDA TRENT
High
Society

Silhouette Special Edition

Published by Silhouette Books New York

America's Publisher of Contemporary Romance

SILHOUETTE BOOKS
300 East 42nd St., New York, N.Y. 10017

Copyright © 1987 by Dan and Lynda Trent

ISBN: 0-373-09378-0

First Silhouette Books printing April 1987

Books by Lynda Trent

Silhouette Intimate Moments

Designs #36
Taking Chances #68
Castles in the Sand #134

Silhouette Desire

The Enchantment #201
Simple Pleasures #223

Silhouette Special Edition

High Society #378

LYNDA TRENT

started writing romances at the insistence of a friend, but it was her husband who provided moral support whenever her resolve flagged. Now husband and wife are both full-time writers, and despite the ups and downs of this demanding career, they love every— well, *almost* every—minute of it.

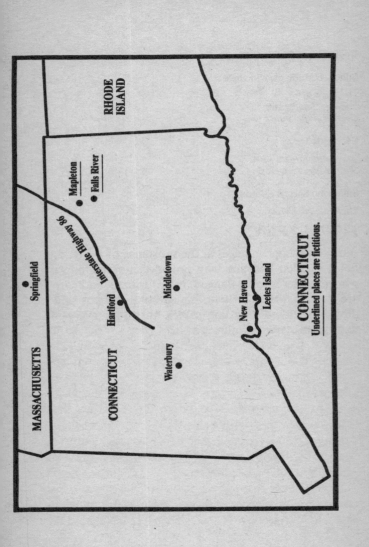

Chapter One

Sheila Danforth leaned forward in an effort to peer through the blinding snowstorm as her gloved hands gripped the steering wheel. She had been foolish to try to beat the storm home, she realized belatedly. The storm had come whipping in over Connecticut's wooded terrain much faster than she would ever have believed possible. Nervously she upbraided herself for putting too much stock in the weather forecast. Late storms like this one were much too unpredictable.

In the glare of her headlights, the road wavered, appeared, and disappeared again. Howling gusts of freezing rain and snow swirled around her. Sheila slowed the car to a mere crawl and tried not to panic as sleet beat a tattoo against her Mercedes's windshield. Was she near the sharp curve that signaled the approach to Falls River? The storm had confused her, and she was no longer sure where she was.

A capricious gust cleared her windshield for a tantalizing moment, and Sheila pulled the steering wheel to the left. She had been almost off the pavement and hadn't even realized it. Surely the curve in the road couldn't be too far ahead!

A large tree, still gaunt with the nakedness of winter, loomed near, so she veered away from it. She must have drifted off the road again, she realized nervously. No tree would be growing so near the roadway. Her windshield wipers strained to clear the fresh, wet snow, but the glass was beginning to glaze over with a thin sheet of ice. Sheila jiggled the knob that controlled the defroster. It didn't seem to be working properly.

A sheen of nervous perspiration slicked her upper lip and forehead in spite of the cold. The heater wasn't acting right either, she realized with a groan. The irony of the whole affair was that she had been to Mapleton to get the heater fixed and that was how she happened to get caught in the storm. No matter what her sister-in-law Estelle Simon said about the inadequacies of Falls River's mechanics, she should have had the problem fixed in town. Or better yet, stayed home instead.

Snow-covered bushes loomed into view on her left, and with a spurt of terror Sheila realized the car had wandered across the oncoming lane and off the shoulder. As quickly as she dared, she righted her course. Fortunately she seemed to be alone on the road. Everyone else must have found shelter or been wise enough not to venture out. Trying not to cry,

Sheila told herself that she couldn't be too far from town. If she could only see the lights of a house, she could head there and wait it out.

All at once her vision was filled with the black bulk of a fir, and she swerved, but over the shriek of the storm she heard the sickening grind of tree limbs against her hood. The Mercedes lurched at an angle into the soft snow of a ditch and came to a complete stop.

The abrupt halt threw Sheila forward against the wheel, and for a stunned moment she was afraid to move. Putting the car in reverse, she pressed the accelerator and heard the whine of tires spinning futilely in the snow. Not letting herself dwell on her plight, Sheila tried to move forward in low gear. Again the wheels complained as they failed to grip the ground, and the car settled lower into the drift.

After a few more efforts, Sheila sat back and stared at the fir that blocked her view. Its branches shook and tossed in the wind, sending a shiver through her. She had no idea what to do. The car wasn't about to budge.

Sheila flexed her expensively gloved hands and wished she had had more sense than to listen to Estelle. Not knowing what else to do, she tried to open her door, but it didn't give, even when she put her weight against it. Pressing the electric window lever with her left hand, Sheila caught the fingertips of the other glove in her teeth and pulled it off.

As the window lowered, snow swirled into the car and freezing rain stung her face, making her eyes water. She reached out and felt for the outside door latch but discovered that a sheath of ice had already formed over the handle. Now she was literally frozen in.

Hastily she raised the window and pulled on her glove as the ailing heater tried to rewarm the air inside. The snowflakes that had blown in melted and beaded on her fur parka and in the strands of her shoulder-length dark brown hair. What was she going to do? She couldn't be far off the road, but no one would find her in a storm like this. She glanced at her diamond-rimmed watch. By now her maid had gone home. No one was left to know she hadn't arrived safely.

She read the gas gauge and was relieved to see it still indicated almost a full tank. At least she could keep the engine running and the heater on. Again she strained to peer through the storm. She simply couldn't believe this was happening to her. Snuggling deeper into her parka, she wondered if she could possibly be in as much danger as she thought.

Mike Barlow shifted into low gear as his tow truck pressed into the brunt of the storm. All afternoon he had been rescuing those people who were either foolhardy or too ignorant to know they should have stayed indoors in weather like this. He didn't mind. Freak snowstorms often meant cash in his pocket. Not that he gouged motorists like a few of his buddies did. They got around the regulated towing charges by stopping at a stranded car and claiming they were on their way to a call but would be back in an hour or so. Almost always the helpless motorist would offer a handsome tip to buy priority. Mike could never stoop to such a level.

Not that he was a saint. Mike Barlow had spent his share of nights in the Falls River jail for hell-raising, but basically he had his scruples. Besides, he made enough money between the tow truck and his garage to earn his living. That was good enough for him.

Mike had worked his way north on 86 to the border between Connecticut and Massachusetts, then had headed back toward Hartford. By now, the highway was virtually free of traffic, and what few cars he saw were all still moving, though at a snail's pace. When he reached the exit for Highway 32, Mike turned off his police scanner and headed south, then turned left onto the smaller road that lead to Falls River.

When it was too dark or too deep to tow any more cars, he would go home and start a fire in his fireplace. Dinner would be a frozen pizza—pepperoni with cheese—and a beer. Afterward he would watch a little TV and turn in early. Mike lived alone, but he was seldom lonely. He had never met a woman who could persuade him to sacrifice his solitude. He seriously doubted that such a woman even existed. Not that he was opposed to a trial run every so often.

He didn't wear a watch because he didn't own one, but judging from the change in the color of the snow from white to a dull blue-gray, he surmised that night was drawing near. Mike had never had much use for watches. A big utility clock in his garage let him know when it was time to close the shop for the day, and he had an alarm clock beside his bed that he usually remembered to wind. That was about as regulated as he wanted his life to be.

Whistling to the static-filled radio music, Mike headed back to town. He had always enjoyed storms of any kind. In celebration of this one he would break out a chocolate bar for dessert. He might even forgo television and try to coax a few new tunes out of his old guitar.

Sheila's forehead was puckered in a frown as she tried yet again to start her car. It had been running just fine—the gas gauge still showed nearly half a tank—but the engine had simply quit. Maybe snow was blocking the tail pipe. Something had caused the engine to stall. When it came to automobiles, she knew next to nothing—only enough to drive to the next town for a minor repair job and get caught in the worst storm of the year. She muttered an expletive that she doubted any Danforth had uttered since the beginning of time. There was no longer any way of denying that she was in real danger.

The starter struggled weakly, then whined to silence. On the next try the engine barely turned over at all, and her dashboard lights dimmed to near extinction. Sheila turned off the ignition and leaned her forehead on her hands against the steering wheel.

Outside the windshield, the fir tree loomed like a black cliff that was scarcely discernible from the darkening sky. Without the motor's low hum, Sheila could hear the wind sighing and whispering as it threaded through the green needles and gusted puffs of snow to cover the hood of her white car. The storm's rage had slackened somewhat, but now it was too dark to see anything, as if there was anything to see but an empty road through the middle of a forest.

Not knowing what else to do, Sheila turned the key and turned on her headlights. The fir's rough bark, with tracings of snow in the crevices, was now lit up. At least, she thought, if anyone came along, they would see her lights.

With the engine off, the faulty heater was totally useless, and the car's warmth was fading fast. Sheila wondered what she should do to stay warm. She kept an old quilt in the car, but it was in the trunk, and she was frozen into the car.

She checked the backseat, but it was empty as she knew it would be. She had never been one to toss things into her car and leave them there in disarray. In their short marriage, George had impressed upon her that a Danforth didn't do that sort of thing. Numbly she reflected that she hadn't thought of George in weeks, maybe months. And then only when Estelle had brought him up. Theirs had not been an ideal marriage.

Now here she was, about to become a statistic just like George.

She curled her feet beneath her and refused to let her thoughts take that track. She would get out of this. Sheila had always been a survivor; she didn't buckle easily. All the same, she wished the car wasn't chilling so rapidly and that night wasn't falling so quickly. Miserably she wrapped her arms around herself in the middle of the glove-leather seat and wished she could at least get to that quilt.

Mike belted out the lyrics to a golden oldie playing on the radio. Night was falling, and he had switched on his lights. With the truck's four-wheel drive, he had no problems traversing the accumulating snow. It was just a matter of keeping on until he reached town. He could almost smell that wood smoke and pizza.

Ahead was the sharp curve at the outskirts of town. Past that the road dipped low into the valley carved by the river for which the town was named.

He sang the song's chorus with more volume than accuracy as he carefully took the sharp curve. Breaking off in midnote, Mike frowned. Had he seen something back there in the bushes? Surely not. But still, on a night like this, it was possible.

Drifting to a stop, Mike put his truck in reverse and backed up. Again his headlights caught a red reflection. Leaning forward, he strained to see if it was a car's taillight or merely a reflector marking the curve. Twice he almost drove on, but finally he eased the truck onto the shoulder to get a better look.

The Mercedes was white and almost buried in bushes, which explained why he had almost missed seeing it. Since no steam curled from the tail pipe, Mike concluded that it must be abandoned. No one would sit in there without the heater on. Again he considered driving away.

On the other hand, if the driver had hit that fir at any speed at all, he might still be inside, unconscious. Mike thought that was pretty unlikely from the tilt of the car. A crash would likely have turned the car at a different angle. Still, since he was there, he thought he'd better check it out.

Mike pulled his double-knit cap down over his ears and thrust his hands into his fleece-lined work gloves. Zipping up his thick coat, he got out and walked toward the car. He pulled a bush aside and read the personalized license plate—DAN4TH.

"Damn," he muttered. He glanced briefly at the darkened windshield, spotted no occupants, and let the bush slap back against the car. Wouldn't you know it would be a Danforth keeping him from his dinner and the warmth of his fireside. Unreasonably irritated, he turned and strode back toward his truck. Let someone else take a chance on getting mired in the drifts while they hauled the vehicle. He had better things to do than to haul a Danforth's abandoned Mercedes back to town.

Sheila was so cold that she wasn't sure what was real and what was a dream. At times she seemed to be drifting a little above herself as if this were all happening to someone else. When she first saw the headlights, she had blinked and stared at their reflection in her rearview mirror. A car out here in the storm? She had to be hallucinating. To move at all was too much of an effort, so she remained crouched on the seat and waited.

The lights were obscured briefly as if someone was walking in front of them, then she heard footsteps crunching in the icy snow. Sheila's head jerked up as she heard a bush scrape away from the car and snap back again. Someone *was* out there!

She waved and tried to make a sound, but her throat seemed to be closed with emotion. Then, aghast, she heard the footsteps withdrawing. Again she tried to force open the door, but it was useless. She pressed the lever to lower the window, but the battery was drained from leaving on her lights.

Desperation finally brought her to her senses, and with one simple motion she leaned into the horn with all her weight.

Mike stopped dead in his tracks. Someone was in there!

He waded back through the snow and, seeing a woman's face pressed against the driver's window, he tried to make her understand that he was going to get her out. She was crying and making such a fuss, however, that he doubted she heard him. Mike went back to his truck and backed it around until the hoist was as near the stranded car as he dared. He pulled the heavy chain out and attached it under the car, then returned to the truck to haul the automobile out of the ditch.

The lone woman waved frantically as Mike walked over to the door. Although he yanked on it with all his strength, he was no match for the ice. Mike growled as he went back to the truck for the propane heater. Leave it to a Danforth to get stuck on a night like this and get frozen in as well. He wished some other tow truck had been the lucky finder.

At last he warmed the door enough to open it and was able to wrench it ajar. The woman scrambled out as if she thought he might leave her behind. He almost wished he could. She was shaking visibly and crying as she tilted her head back to look up at him. He wasn't sure which one she was, but it didn't matter. They were all alike.

"Thank you," Sheila gasped between sobs. "Thank you! I was afraid no one would come by. I could have frozen to death by morning." She had pulled the fur hood of her coat over her head and was holding it close about her face.

With so little available light, Mike couldn't make out her features. "It's nothing. Just doing my job."

Sheila glanced at the snowy expanse of roadway. "If you could jump-start the car and get me on the road," she said doubtfully, "I think I can..."

"Get stuck again," he finished for her. "Look, lady, this is a blizzard. You can't go driving around in weather like this." He looked up at the snowy air. "It's getting worse again."

"Can I ride back to town with you?"

"Sure, why not?" he said grudgingly. "I may start a taxi service next."

"Wait, I forgot my purse," Sheila called out to him as he strode off. As she grabbed her bag and slammed her car door, she heard him grumbling something, but she couldn't make out the words. She hoped he didn't turn out to be a nut or something. No one else was around to rescue her from her rescuer.

Stumbling through the drifts, Sheila hurried to the truck as fast as she could. By the way the man was acting, he might be as apt to drive off and leave her as not.

Mike was waiting for her, though impatiently. He saw her flounder in a deep drift, and he smiled sardonically; the boots she was wearing probably cost her well over a hundred dollars, and they were less serviceable than his bargain-brand ones. With a sigh, he leaned across the seat and opened the door for her. If they didn't hurry, there was a chance they couldn't get through the valley with snow coming down like this.

The light came on as the door opened, and she climbed in. For the first time their eyes met and held in fascinated amazement.

She was younger than he had thought. Maybe in her late twenties to early thirties. Her brown hair slowed in thick skeins about her creamy face, and her eyes were large and green. Her thick black lashes glistened with melting snowflakes. Her cheeks were rosy from the cold, as were her moist, slightly parted lips. Framed in the hood of luxurious red fox was the most beautiful face he had ever seen.

Nor could Sheila look away from him. Rather than the gruff old man she had taken him to be, he was young—perhaps slightly younger than herself. Thick dark gold hair showed beneath his rough navy cap. His eyes were bright brown with flecks of clear amber. The small scar on one lean cheek didn't detract from his handsomeness.

"Hello," she said softly, as if her voice came from far away. "My name is Sheila Danforth."

After a pause, he said, "I'm Mike Barlow. Shut the door. You're letting out all the warm air."

Chapter Two

Sheila slammed the door of the tow truck and burrowed deeper into her parka as the truck's heater worked to dispel the cold. Behind her she saw her abandoned Mercedes in the snowy bank. "Do you think it will be all right? I forgot to lock the door."

Mike snorted and shoved his gearshift into low. "I doubt there are many car thieves out tonight. Once this snow stops, we'll be out to tow your car into town first thing."

Sheila's quick glance at him told her he was determined to stay surly. She edged closer to the truck's door. She had no option but to trust him to get her to safety, but she wasn't at all sure she was any better off with him than in the blizzard. Unconsciously she hugged her purse to her chest as if for protection.

Mike could see her out of the corner of his eye. The way she was hanging on to that purse, one would think she had diamonds in there. Maybe she did, he thought with disgust. She was a Danforth, after all, and she had plenty of diamonds on her fingers. Maybe she carried her extras in that purse. The idea almost made him smile.

"How far is it to town?" she asked.

"Not far."

"A mile? Five miles?"

"How can you be lost at the edge of your own town?" he retorted.

"I got so disoriented in that storm. For the last few miles I could hardly see the road." For a panicky moment she couldn't tell whether he was taking her toward town or away from it, as he maneuvered onto the scarcely definable road.

"No wonder you ended up in a ditch."

His tone didn't encourage conversation, so she stared out her window at the snow-studded sky. They crested a hill and started down the incline. Sheila caught her breath as the wheels hit a patch of ice and fishtailed for a moment before again finding traction. Her involuntary gasp made him grin sarcastically. Sheila tried her best to ignore him.

Mike's concentration returned to the road beneath him as the truck skidded again when he began down the hill. Ahead he could see the lights from the Quick Stop Cafe, Falls River's farthest outpost. On the opposite hill were a few scattered lights from outlying houses. If they could top the next hill, Falls River would be clearly visible. But first they had to cross the river.

The drifts deepened as they neared the bottom of the valley. The broad expanse of Falls River flowed through the snow like a black ribbon, illuminated by the truck's headlights, then disappearing into the distant darkness. The bridge was low and narrow with what now seemed to be a very flimsy guardrail between it and the water.

Mike slowed and studied the lower valley before trying to drive into it. The road here was buried under drifts of snow, and even from this distance he could see the bridge was coated with ice.

"What's wrong?" his passenger asked fearfully. "Why are we stopping?"

Mike put the truck in reverse, not bothering to answer. He hadn't expected the valley to become impassable so soon. Carefully he backed up the way they had come as he considered his alternatives.

"Why are you backing up?" Her voice was trembling as she gripped the door handle convulsively. "Why aren't you going forward?"

Leaning his forearms on the steering wheel, Mike frowned at her. "We can't get through there. Look at those drifts."

"I thought trucks like this could go anywhere. They can, can't they?"

He turned toward the faint lights of the Quick Stop Cafe and didn't deign to answer her.

"Where are we going? Look, if it's a question of money…" Sheila's voice trailed off. Perhaps it wasn't such a good idea to let him know she was carrying money.

"Listen, lady, maybe you don't mind risking your neck on an icy bridge, but I'm not going to."

"But where—"

"Will you quit asking questions? It's hard enough to drive in this storm without carrying on a conversation at the same time."

Sheila scrunched down in the corner. He sounded almost dangerous, and she couldn't recall ever being so afraid. Tears stung her eyes, but she batted them back. She wasn't about to show any weakness in front of this man.

As they slipped and careened into the weak circle of light put out by the single bulb over the cafe's entrance, she scarcely dared to breathe. The building was low and square; its name was emblazoned in red and blue across the plate-glass window. She had seen countless cafes like this, usually with the parking lot jammed with trucks. Never had she considered stopping at one.

Mike shut off the engine and got out. The blast of frigid air rushing into the truck made Sheila jump, and she watched him for a minute before she realized that he planned to go inside. Fumbling with her door handle to open it, she hurried after him.

He didn't acknowledge her presence with even so much as a glance. After trying to open the locked door, he headed for the window and she had to dodge out of his way. He cupped his hands around his face and peered into the dark interior. Then he pounded on the window and looked in again.

"Is anyone in there?" she asked as she shivered.

Mike turned away and hunched his shoulders against the raw wind as he strode around the corner.

Sheila clutched her hood about her face and tried to hurry after him. The heels of her boots sank in the

way radio in your truck and let her know you're all right."

"Nobody is expecting me." He went back to the kitchen and started rummaging through the containers of food.

Sheila stood in the doorway, warily watching him. She couldn't decide if she should be afraid of him or not.

"Are you hungry?" he asked over his shoulder. "What do you want?"

"I don't know. What is there to choose from?"

"Lady, this is a restaurant. Pick anything," he said in exasperation. "I doubt Sam has any truffles, and I'm pretty sure he's out of caviar, but I imagine there is something in here you could manage to put down." His tone of voice belied his words.

"I'd love a hamburger," she replied after a brief hesitation. "Do you think we'll get in trouble for cooking in here?"

Mike couldn't repress his laugh. "Anybody who eats at the Quick Stop is taking his life into his own hands." He nodded toward the wall of refrigerators. "Get the lettuce and cheese. They're behind the second door." He went to the first door and got two frozen hamburger patties.

Sheila pulled off her gloves, then gathered some lettuce, cheese, and tomato slices. "I mean I wonder if this counts as breaking and entering."

"It probably counts, but Sam won't press charges. We're friends. He'll even help me fix his door. Are there any pickles?"

Sheila found the pickle slices and a jar of mustard as Mike tossed the frozen patties onto the heated cooking grill. She hoped it was more sanitary than the black surface indicated, but she wasn't about to complain. Instead, she searched for buns.

As the building warmed up, Sheila unbuttoned her fur parka and let the hood fall back. Beneath, she wore a suede pantsuit. At her neck, she had knotted a colorful silk scarf with a geometric design.

Mike looked at her for a moment, then turned back to the grill. "That's not a very practical outfit for going out in a snowstorm."

"I hadn't planned to be in one."

He turned the patties and said, "Why were you on the road, anyway? Didn't you pay any attention to the travel warnings?"

"By the time the warnings were posted I was in Mapleton. My car heater has been acting up, and I took it over to be repaired."

"What's wrong with the repair shop in Falls River?" he asked defensively.

"My brother-in-law says the one in Mapleton is better." Her voice faltered as she saw his frown.

Mike slapped the meat onto the bun and shoved it at her. "Listen, lady, there's nothing wrong with my shop. Mapleton just charges more and makes people think they get their money's worth with a fancy wait-. ing area. That's all."

"I didn't know you owned the shop here. I didn't mean to offend you. And my name is Sheila. Sheila Danforth."

"I know your name." Mike turned off the grill and shouldered by her to go into the dining room. Not looking back to see whether she was following, Mike pulled a bag of chips off the dispenser rack and sat down in a red vinyl booth.

With a frown, Sheila helped herself to chips and joined him in the booth. "I don't know why you're being so unfriendly," she chided as he put salt and pepper on his hamburger.

"Yes, you do."

"If it's money, I fully intend to pay you for all the trouble you've gone to."

Mike leaned forward, angrily shifting in his seat. "Don't start throwing your money at me. I don't need it, and I sure don't want it. Not Danforth money."

Swallowing the bite of burger, Sheila demanded, "What's wrong with Danforth money?"

Mike chewed in silence for a minute. "Maybe you didn't catch my name. I'm Mike *Barlow*."

"So?"

"So this is the longest time anyone of my family and anyone of your family has had anything to do with the other in ninety years. You know that."

"I know there has been some problem between our families, but—"

"Problem, hell. We've been feuding since the turn of the century."

"But why?"

"Don't hand me that. Every Danforth that's been born since the feud started has been taught to hate us Barlows."

"In the first place, I haven't been told to hate anybody," she retorted stiffly. "In the second, I wasn't born a Danforth. I married one."

Again Mike was quiet, watching her while he ate. "Then I guess Mr. Danforth must be mighty worried about you." Mike thought to himself that if he had a wife who looked like Sheila, he wouldn't want her lost in a snowstorm.

"No. No one is worrying about me. I'm a widow."

"Then you must have been married to George Danforth, the doctor," he stated rather than asked.

"You seem to know quite a lot about the family," she answered in surprise.

"I read the paper. A Danforth can't sneeze in Falls River without the society page covering the event."

Now Sheila was silent. After a while, she said, "You never answered me when I asked why our families dislike each other so."

Mike studied her thoughtfully with his golden brown gaze as he finished the last bite of his hamburger. "You really don't know?"

"No, I don't, but I'd really like to."

"Nearly a hundred years ago my great-grandfather had a business here. Not a big one at first, but it grew. Before long he was the leading furniture builder in this area. Beautiful work—walnut, cherry, maple. He was especially well known for his inlaid work. It was all done by hand, then he hand-polished the entire piece."

"I don't think I've ever seen any of his furniture," Sheila said softly. Mike's voice had sounded so vulnerable when he spoke of his family.

"No, I wouldn't imagine you had. He took that business and built a small fortune for himself. Then Zachary Danforth came to town." Mike's voice hardened. "At first we tried to help out the newcomer, introduced him around, in fact. Then he set up a furniture business of his own. Only he mass-produced his furniture. That meant he could make it faster and sell it cheaper. For a while we held our own, but before long people began to prefer the mass-produced line. Like I say, it was cheaper.''

Sheila was quiet. The Danforth furniture factory was still active and very profitable.

"In a few years time the Barlow line couldn't continue to compete. We went bankrupt. It's said that old Zachary Danforth stood on the street and laughed the day the bank repossessed our family business.''

"It sounds like Barlow babies are the ones taught to carry on the feud," Sheila observed. "Like I said, I never even heard the story before."

"And that's why," Mike began his summation as if she hadn't spoken, "I drive a tow truck and you drive a Mercedes."

Sheila reached for a paper napkin and wiped her lips and fingers. "If the story is true..."

"It is."

"...then I don't blame you in the least."

Mike leaned forward. "Say that again?"

"I think your great-grandfather had a perfect right to hate great-grandfather Danforth. Even their children might have felt justified. But that was a long time ago. Don't you think it's time to end it?"

"I can't believe I'm hearing this."

"If you ask me, all the hard feelings are on your side. I certainly have nothing against your family. Now that you've rescued me, I think we ought to declare a truce."

"A truce?" he asked incredulously.

"Why not?"

Mike slid out of the booth and tossed the remains of his food in a waste receptacle. "Do you want coffee?"

"I'd love anything hot." She finished cleaning off the table and sat on a counter stool as she watched him prepare a pot of coffee. Leaning her forearms on the scuffed Formica countertop, she prompted, "Well?"

"Well what?"

"Are we going to continue the feud or not?"

When he turned, she was smiling at him. Again he was struck by her beauty. Against the apricot tint of her skin, her eyes glowed like jewels. There was an auburn gleam in the highlights of her dark hair. Her teeth were white and perfectly straight, and her lips were sensuously full. If she were anyone but a Danforth, Mike knew he would be falling all over himself to get to know her better. "I guess we could call a halt to it for a while and see how it works out," he ventured.

"Naturally I wouldn't ask you to do something as drastic as calling off a feud if it didn't feel comfortable to you," she teased. "Let's just try it on a trial basis."

Trying to decide if she was baiting him, Mike nodded. "We could do that." He turned back to pour each of them a mug of coffee.

"You go first," Sheila said. "Tell me about yourself. Are you married?"

"I told you nobody is waiting up for me."

"That's not the same as 'I'm not married,'" she reminded him.

"Then, I'm not married." He leaned back against the service counter and watched her over the rim of his coffee mug.

"Are you engaged?"

"Nope. I was once. When I was in the air force, I was stationed in West Germany and became engaged to the daughter of one of the sergeants."

"It didn't work out?"

"She was an army brat and couldn't imagine any other life. I wanted to get out of the service and settle down. We finally called it off. No emotional scars, no lasting regrets. What about you?"

"I'm from Kentucky, originally. I met George when I was a freshman at Bryn Mawr and he was doing his residency at a hospital in Philadelphia. After I graduated, we were married here in Falls River where he was practicing medicine. His speciality, as you probably know, was cardiac surgery. What you probably didn't know is that his other specialty was Scotch."

"I didn't know."

"It never made the papers. Anyway, he had been drinking heavily the night he died and was entirely to blame for the automobile accident. Thank goodness no one else was seriously injured."

"You didn't have to tell me about his drinking. Why did you?"

"It's part of the truce. You can't have a friendship if nothing is risked." She met his eyes frankly. "I would like to be your friend."

Mike studied her for a long time. "I can't figure you out. You aren't at all the way I pictured the Danforth family."

"I told you, I only married into it."

"How long were you married?"

"Five years."

"And he's been dead about a year."

"About that."

"You must have married young. Six years ago I was barely out of high school."

Sheila made a noncommittal sound. She had just turned twenty-four when she and George had married, and that made her five years older than Mike. She saw no reason to point that out.

Mike poured them each more coffee and slowly walked back around the counter. Did she have any idea how desirable he found her? "What about you and George? Are you still mourning him? I see you still wear his ring."

Sheila glanced down at her left hand. She hadn't guessed he would notice such a thing. "No. No, I'm not missing him."

"Then why the ring?"

"I just never got around to taking it off." She fingered the platinum, and the cluster of diamonds sparkled with their familiar fire. Why *was* she wearing it, she wondered. "I guess it's more or less expected that I wear it to keep up appearances."

"Do you always do what's expected of you?" He slid into the nearest booth and propped his back against the far wall.

"Not always," she said defensively. In order to avoid conflict, Sheila was more apt than not to give in. Afterward she always berated herself.

He smiled at her as if he didn't quite believe her answer.

"Does your family still live here?" she asked, to change the subject.

"I'm all that's left of my immediate family. I have a few distant cousins, most of whom live in Falls River. What about your family back in Kentucky?"

She shrugged. "We aren't close. George's family sort of took me in when we married." Actually Estelle, George's sister, had tried to take her over, not in. Sheila always felt like a coerced outsider, but she had no intention of letting Mike know that. The one thing her parents, and later George and the Danforths, had stressed above all was family unity. The family, as a buffer against outsiders, had always been a protection, even though she had never really fitted in.

"And that makes you a Danforth."

"I guess it does."

"Are you dating anyone in particular?" he asked, as if her answer didn't matter much one way or the other to him.

"No. No one in particular. Are you?"

"Not right now."

Sheila wondered if he was teasing her or if he really had no one special. She found it hard to believe that someone with so much charisma could be completely unattached. She reminded herself that this wasn't any of her business.

Outside the window, the storm still beat against the building. An icy wind howled around the eaves as if seeking a way to get in. Sheila shivered even though the room was almost warm enough now for her to remove her coat.

"Are you still cold?"

"No, it's the storm. They always make me nervous."

"I like storms. The wilder, the better. Especially when I'm inside and can sit back in comfort and just watch. Don't worry. This will blow itself out tonight."

"Don't you worry that the lines will go down and leave us with no electricity?"

"What if they do? The heat is butane. We won't get cold. Besides, Sam has never had much trouble with electricity."

She still looked worried, so Mike reached across the Formica tabletop and covered her hand with his own. Hers was so small that his engulfed it, and her skin was smooth and cool. Her fingers felt as delicate as porcelain within his. Their eyes met in a startled glance as something tangible seemed to jump from one to the other. They hastily withdrew their hands.

"I think I had better be sure the back door is shut," Mike mumbled as he climbed out of the booth. All at once the arrangement seemed far too intimate.

"I'll wash the stove," Sheila volunteered quickly. From his abrupt departure, she wondered if he had been aware of the spark she had felt when he'd touched her.

Chiding herself for acting like a moonstruck child, Sheila went to the huge sink and searched for soap and a scouring pad. George had been dead for a year, and even before that, intimacy between them had dwindled to almost nothing. Not that they hadn't loved each other, she assured herself automatically, but he hadn't been a physically demonstrative man. Some people just showed their love more aesthetically than others. Unfortunately Sheila was the physical type, and she missed having someone to hold her. Up until now, she hadn't realized how much she had missed it.

The griddle's surface was baked black, and no amount of scrubbing would change that, so Sheila did the best she could, then rinsed the surface. She turned to find Mike watching her from the doorway. Hoping he hadn't divined any of her thoughts, she dried the griddle and then her hands.

"Want to listen to music?"

"You have a radio?"

"Only in my truck. But there's a jukebox in the dining room."

"Yes, I'll be right in." She wanted a few seconds to collect herself. Taking her purse, she went into the rest room and brushed her hair and put on lip gloss. Thoughtfully she looked at herself in the mirror. In her own opinion, she wasn't particularly pretty, though she always tried to look her best. That was why she had put on the lip gloss and brushed her hair until it was gleaming. No other reason. The rest room however, had no heat, so she didn't linger.

The jukebox was going by the time she rejoined him. The song was one from several years before, and Sheila reflected that this Sam person didn't bother to keep his jukebox up-to-date. Or maybe his patrons just didn't care. She felt a twinge of guilt at the snobbish thought—it sounded just like something Estelle would say.

She sat in a chair at one of the square tables, and he sat at the table next to it, as if not sharing a tabletop might reduce the intimacy.

"What are your interests?" Sheila asked when the silence grew between them. "What do you like to do?"

"You mean like a hobby? I don't have much time for things like that. The garage keeps me pretty busy. Not everybody drives to Mapleton for repairs." He frowned as he spun the salt shaker between his fingers. "Sorry. I didn't mean that the way it sounded."

"I didn't take it that way." She told herself not to seem so eager to please. He would think she had designs on him or something.

Still twirling the salt shaker, Mike said, "I like vintage cars. If I had a hobby, that would be what I'd choose."

"You mean to restore them?"

"Yeah. I own a couple that I work on whenever I have time. One is a 1965 Mustang. They're very popular these days. The other is a 1930 Ford coupe."

"Have you ever considered doing that full-time? I should think old cars like that would be worth a great deal of money."

"Sure, they bring a lot when you're through, but do you have any idea what it would cost to get started in something like that? I don't have Danforth money," he countered with a frown.

"But once you got a start, wouldn't it be more profitable than a regular garage?"

"Sure it would. But the bank doesn't see it that way. Without a loan I can't set up, so it's still a dream."

"Maybe someday."

The song ended and another began.

"What about you? Surely you have hobbies."

"I paint a little and like to do needlework. I belong to the garden club and a literary group that meets once a month."

"What's a literary group?"

"We read and then discuss books. Don't look at me like that—it's enjoyable."

"I'm sure it is."

"Where did you go to school?" she asked, to steer the subject back to him.

"Right here in Falls River."

"But there's no..." she started before she thought better.

"I didn't go to college," he said abruptly. He had always regretted that. When he had said he thought a literary club would be fun, he had meant it. Reading was his primary pastime, and he was self-educated in a broad range of subjects, but he never admitted it. Not to anyone.

The slow strains of the music offered him an escape from the awkward moment. "Dance?" he asked.

Sheila paused, but his eyes were daring her so she nodded. He stood and pushed the table and chairs aside to make room for them. As she stepped into his arms, she realized she had made a big mistake. He had taken off his coat just as she had, and she could feel the hard strength of his muscles beneath the blue chambray shirt. The warmth of his palm against her waist seemed to burn her, and her other hand was lost in his. He was taller than she had realized; the top of her head just grazed his chin. To look at his face, she had to tilt her head back, leaning her body into him.

He was staring down at her as if he were awestruck. She tried to look away as he led her in a dance step, but she was mesmerized by the gold lights in his eyes.

She was being foolish, she told herself over and over. What she was feeling was a simple biological urge brought on by months of abstinence. She would have felt this way no matter what man was holding her. His rugged good looks and that tawny thatch of hair had nothing more to do with it than the way his shoulder muscles rippled under her hand. That ever so comfortable at-home feeling was pure illusion.

Mike felt as if someone had kicked him in the middle. He couldn't breathe, and he sure couldn't turn her loose. She was as light as thistledown in his arms. The desire in her eyes reminded him of bedrooms and firelight. Could real eyelashes be so long and thick? Evidently they could. Her lips were dewy and inviting, as if she had just been kissed.

Against his better judgment, Mike wondered if he should kiss her. A real kiss. The kind that went on forever and led to other things. Silently cursing himself for his foolishness, he was glad when the music ended and he had a valid excuse for stepping away from her. Another minute or so and he couldn't have torn himself free.

Sheila turned away and went back to the booth. Mike jammed his hands into the back pockets of his jeans and headed in the opposite direction. She was a Danforth, damn it!

From across the room they gauged one another, each wondering if the other could possibly feel the same way. The last of the songs finished playing, and the silence was more strained than ever.

Finally Mike went back to the booth and took up his position with his back against the wall and his legs stretched out on the vinyl seat.

Somehow neither felt much like talking.

Chapter Three

Morning dawned beneath a sullen sky. The snow-fall had stopped, but the threat still lingered. Mike and Sheila had fallen asleep in the booth, both crumpled onto their respective seats.

A rough hand grabbed Mike's arm and shook him, none too gently. At once he was awake, his eyes narrowed in alert caution. Two policemen stood beside their table, one glaring at Mike, the other waking Sheila. Mike flexed to ease his cramped muscles, and the policeman tensed.

"What are you doing in here?" one policeman demanded.

"We came in to get out of the storm," Mike explained as he watched Sheila raise her tousled head and blink sleepily.

"Sure," the man said in obvious disbelief. He stepped to the cash register and frowned at it suspiciously.

"Don't I know you?" the other officer asked Mike in an unpleasant voice. "Aren't you Mike Barlow? I think I took you in on a drunk-and-disorderly charge last month."

Mike stretched again and made an exaggerated examination of the policeman. "Yes, I believe that was you."

"Don't get smart-mouthed. Where's the cash out of the drawer?"

Mike's features turned to stone as his amusement changed to defensiveness. "I imagine it's with Sam Threadgill. He's the owner."

Sheila was awake now and staring from one man to another.

"How do you know who owns this place?" the first officer demanded of Mike.

"Sam is a friend of mine. He never leaves cash in the drawer overnight. Call him at home and ask him."

"You seem to have a lot of ready answers. You wouldn't know his number or address, would you?"

Mike sighed. "No. I wouldn't."

"Yet you say he's a friend of yours."

Sheila finally spoke. "Officer, is there a problem?"

"You and your boyfriend broke into this place and sacked out all night. That's the problem." The man scowled at her. "How do I know you two didn't take the money? I have a mind to run you both in."

"That's ridiculous," Sheila objected. "We took no money. We only broke in because we would have frozen otherwise. Tell them, Mike."

"They won't believe us. I've been through this before."

"He sure has. What about you, ma'am. How about showing me some ID?"

Sheila stood up and gathered all the Danforth dignity she could command. "My name is Sheila Danforth. Mrs. George Danforth."

The policemen looked surprised. The other officer paused as he started to haul Mike out of the booth.

"This man found me stranded in a snowbank last night," she informed them in frigid tones. "He saved my life. We were unable to cross the valley by the time we got this far and were forced to stay here."

"On our shift-change sheet this morning I noticed that a Mrs. Simon reported that a Sheila Danforth was missing," the younger officer reminded his partner. "Do you suppose this could be the one?"

Sheila fixed him with a penetrating glare. "There is only one Sheila Danforth." Reaching into her purse, she extracted her driver's license and thrust it at the older of the two.

The officer studied the card for a moment, looking from Sheila to her picture and back again. "I'm sorry, Mrs. Danforth," the man stammered in a very apologetic tone. "We had no idea it was you."

She swept her cool gaze over them both. "You came perilously close to false arrest, both of you."

The older officer's brow furrowed for just a moment in concern before he regained his composure. Mike tried to hide his grin. These two officers were known for harassing suspects. In his last run-in with the law, he had been drunk, but he hadn't been disorderly until they'd begun their strong-arm tactics.

Turning to Mike, Sheila said, "The fact that these policemen are here must mean that the snowplow has been by. We can probably get into town now."

"We'll drive you home, Mrs. Danforth," the older man directed, trying to regain control of the situation. "No trouble at all."

"That won't be necessary," she answered in a nononsense voice. "Mr. Barlow will see me home."

Mike uncoiled his lean frame from the booth and made no effort to hide his amusement as he pulled on his coat and zipped it. Helping Sheila into her coat, Mike nodded to the officers and held the door open for her to pass. As he was leaving, Mike called over his shoulder, "Tell Sam I'll take care of getting his door fixed."

Sheila climbed into the tow truck and said indignantly, "How could they do that? Do you realize they were accusing us of theft!"

"Well, we did break and enter."

"Yes, but *theft*." Then she realized how silly that sounded, and she smiled.

"Lady, you've just seen one difference between being a Danforth and being a Barlow."

Sheila was silent as he started the truck. She was still angry at the injustice.

Mike drove her toward town, and within minutes they were on the familiar streets. "Where to?"

"Home, I guess. Estelle must be worried about me if she called the police."

"I've read your name in the paper, but they didn't print your address," he pointed out.

With a faint blush, Sheila said, "Turn right at the next light. I live at 12 Hazelglen."

"I should have guessed," he replied in recognition of the town's most exclusive street.

Sheila turned her head to study him, but his face was a mask. "We're right back where we started, aren't we?" she accused. "Just because I didn't let those policemen arrest us."

"The point is, you could stop them," he objected.

"If I had known it was important to you, I wouldn't have interfered."

He drove in angry silence for a minute, then said, "I guess that is a pretty dumb reason for me to get mad, isn't it?"

"Yep, pretty dumb," Sheila agreed, but when she smiled he grinned back.

"After I drop you off, I'll go get your car."

"Would you mind checking it out before bringing it home? The heater still doesn't work right and the engine quit running on its own."

"Are you sure you don't want to take it back to Mapleton?" he countered.

"Be nice," she teased, pointing at him in a playful warning.

He smiled. "Okay. I'll take a look at it. But I may be busy towing cars for the rest of today. Could be tomorrow before I can get to it."

"That's fine with me. I'm not about to drive in this snow after last night."

He entered her neighborhood and looked over at her sitting in the seat beside him. "Aren't you concerned that everyone in town will see you riding in a tow truck with my name on it?"

"I'm not nearly as worried about it as you are."

"You know, I like you. Maybe it is time to call off the feud."

She looked at him in surprise. "I thought we already had."

Her house was a big red brick Georgian with white trim and federal-blue shutters. The drive, curving gracefully up from the quiet street, was flanked by tall maple trees, now bare silhouettes against the pale sky. Evergreen hedges, heavily laden with snow, skirted the house and bordered what must be flower gardens beneath the blanket of white. Behind the house was a deep lawn enclosed by a privacy hedge and brick wall.

Mike leaned forward and gazed at the mansion. "One person lives in all that house?"

"I had hoped at one time to fill it with children, but that never happened."

"An entire orphanage wouldn't fill this place. The monthly payments must be awful."

When Sheila didn't respond, he looked at her and said in an accusatory voice, "It's paid for. Right?"

"George got a fantastic deal," she replied defensively.

"I'll bet."

He drove under the covered portico and stopped. For a minute he sat looking at her, not wanting their time together to be over.

"Thank you," Sheila said softly. "For everything."

"My pleasure. It really was."

She was quiet for a minute as she tried to think of some reason to postpone his leaving. "Won't you come in? We could have breakfast."

"You cook?"

"No."

Mike laughed and shook his head. "You have a maid?"

"Right again. And she's a wonderful cook."

"No thanks. I'd better not. I have to get to work."

"Maybe some other time?"

He leaned forward. "You really weren't playing a game last night, were you? I mean, you're as real as you seem to be."

"Of course I am. Aren't you?"

The door at the side of the house opened, and a woman Mike judged to be in her forties stepped out onto the porch. She wore a severely tailored navy suit, and her short hair was frosted to conceal the encroaching gray. Wrapping her arms across her flat breasts against the cold, she frowned at the tow truck. Her expression darkened further when she read the name painted on its side.

"Damn, it's Estelle," Sheila muttered without thinking.

Mike appraised the older woman critically. "Now *that's* a Danforth."

"You're right. About breakfast. I was going to plead and cajole until you gave in, but . . ."

"I'll take a rain check."

A brilliant smile broke over her face. "You will?"

Mike read her gleeful expression with pleasure. "Lady, don't ever play poker or you'll lose your shirt.'' He wondered if she knew what she did to him when she smiled like that.

Estelle marched down the cement steps and rapped sharply on the truck's window. Sheila's smile wavered and left her eyes as she became stiffly polite. "I have to go in."

Perversely Mike opened his door and motioned for her to slide across. After a pause, she complied and climbed out to face Estelle.

"So. You're home and safe at last." The woman was taller than Sheila, and her rigid posture made her seem even more statuesque.

"Estelle, I'd like for you to meet Mike Barlow. Mike, this is George's sister, Estelle Simon."

Mike grinned and held out his hand, knowing exactly what the woman's reaction would be. And she didn't disappoint him.

"Hello," Estelle snapped, her voice colder than the air whipping around them. To Sheila she said, "You might have called. We were worried sick. Where were you?"

"We stayed at the Quick Stop," Mike supplied helpfully.

"It's a cafe," Sheila added.

"I know of no all-night cafes in Falls River."

"We broke in," Mike informed her.

Sheila rolled her eyes at him, then said, "It was that or freeze to death, Estelle."

The woman turned her pale blue eyes on Mike. "You're a Barlow." The words were a sharp accusation.

"That's right. I am."

"I'd love to stand out here and chat," Sheila said hastily, "but it's too cold."

Estelle turned her back on Mike in dismissal and put her arm possessively around Sheila.

"Sorry I can't stay," Mike called out cheerfully to Estelle's back, "but I have to get back to work. I'll give you a call, Sheila." When Estelle's head jerked around, he added with a grin, "About your car." If Sheila wanted to end the feud, he had decided she might as well see what she was up against.

Sheila hurried up the steps and into the house. Of all the people she didn't want to see at the moment, Estelle was on the top of the list.

"What were you doing riding in a tow truck?"

"He brought me home." She just wanted to soak in a hot bath and try to sort out the new emotions Mike had awakened. She nodded a greeting to her maid.

"He's a Barlow! I just hope no one saw you."

"He's also the man who saved my life," Sheila replied testily. "I didn't camp out in the cafe by design, you know. My car skidded off the road in the storm and stalled out. If Mike hadn't come along, I would have died."

"I see you're on a first-name basis."

"Well, after all, Estelle, we spent the night together." She pulled off her coat and handed it to the maid, whose eyes widened at her employer's last words.

"Sheila!"

"Not that sort of together." She ran her fingers through her hair and tried to smooth it into its usual page boy.

"I should certainly hope not," Estelle muttered as the maid hurried away.

"We slept on vinyl seats on opposite sides of a booth, with a wide tabletop separating us," Sheila retorted. "What *could* we do in a case like that?"

Estelle looked as shocked as if Sheila had just confessed to a dire scandal. A thought crossed Sheila's mind that perhaps Estelle had more imagination than she had given her credit for. "Nothing happened," she repeated.

"Marie," Estelle called out to the maid, "we'll have coffee in the morning room."

"In the den, Marie," Sheila countermanded. "Honestly, Estelle, I don't order your maid around."

Estelle ignored Sheila's observation.

The two women walked into the oak-paneled den, and Sheila sank into the leather cushions of her favorite overstuffed chair. Estelle sat on the couch and wiped imaginary lint from one of the needlepoint pillows. "You've made more changes in here, I see."

Sheila glanced at the bookshelf where George's medical books had been. She'd recently replaced them with her collection of novels. "Don't worry. I didn't get rid of George's books. I boxed them up and put them in the attic." Marie entered with a tray of coffee and sweet rolls, and Sheila thanked her before pouring Estelle and herself a cup. "As for the guns, I sold those."

Estelle whirled and glared at the wall above the couch where George's gun rack had hung. "You certainly aren't losing any time, are you?" she observed tartly.

"George has been dead over a year," Sheila said in a gentler voice. "I live here alone now. Wouldn't you make a few changes if you were in my position?"

"No. If I were the one in the position of having had the incredible good fortune to marry into a family such as the Danforths, I would uphold that title and all those traditions to my death."

Sheila hid her amusement from years of practice. "I don't want to live in a shrine, Estelle. That went out in Victorian times."

"Make a joke of it. In the meantime, go against the family wishes and ride in a tow truck belonging to a Barlow."

"George never told me not to ride in a tow truck with a Barlow," Sheila replied as she leaned back and sipped her coffee. "Besides, Mike Barlow is a very nice person."

"But he's a Barlow." Estelle sniffed disdainfully. "They're nothing but trash."

"Is it true they owned a furniture business here before great-grandfather Zachary opened his factory?"

"They had some little fly-by-night operation." Estelle waved her ring-encrusted hand, and the diamonds glittered.

"How's Ed?" Sheila asked to change the subject.

"Half out of his mind with worry over you. I'll call him in a minute." She replaced her half-empty cup, and Sheila felt a revulsion at the crinkled crescent of red lipstick left on the rim. Estelle fished a package of cigarettes and a lighter out of her purse. Flicking the lighter, she said, "Where are your ashtrays, dear?"

"I got rid of them since I don't smoke."

"What about your guests?" Estelle queried crossly as she put away her unlit cigarette and lighter.

"I guess they won't smoke here," Sheila answered. She was determined not to back down on this issue.

Estelle snapped her purse shut and tried to carefully gauge her next words. Ever since George died, unexpectedly leaving everything to Sheila, Estelle had been in a tiff. His money was Danforth money, and as such should have gone to a Danforth—namely herself. "I guess you're wondering why I came over," she began in a sweeter voice.

"I assumed you came out of concern for me."

"Well, of course that, too. Also I wanted to discuss the endowment fund."

"What endowment fund?"

"The one in George's name, naturally. I've had Ed look into the legalities in his law firm, and I believe we have a perfect solution."

"Solution to what?"

Ignoring her, Estelle said, "I know you aren't interested in such things, but that's no problem. The way Ed wants to set it up, the fund will be in George's name, since it will be started with his money—a memorial fund, you see—and I will be the administrator since you dislike dealing with money affairs."

"I never said I disliked dealing with money. I've said before that I don't agree to the endowment fund idea." Sheila poured herself another cup of coffee and bit into a sweet roll. "These are delicious. Have one?"

"No, thank you," Estelle said disdainfully. "I prefer to watch my weight. Now about this fund. Let me explain it to you."

Sheila kept a polite expression on her face as she usually did when Estelle tried this tack. She had no intention of giving away her money, but she was frequently amused at Estelle's many and varied approaches to get at it. As ploys went, this was one of the better ones. Not only would Sheila give up the Danforth money, but it would be earmarked as a memorial to George, and Estelle would have control of it. Sheila wondered idly why Estelle never accepted her as a Danforth—in spite of Estelle's numerous protestations that she had—and most amazing of all, why George had. Even during their ardent courtship, when things were the best ever, Sheila had never viewed herself as Danforth material.

Because she had inherited money from her own family, Sheila had never been in awe of the Danforth fortune. Still, money was a lovely security blanket, and Sheila had no inclination toward giving it away. Besides, being a wife to Dr. George Danforth had been a difficult task; in her opinion, she had earned the money.

She waited until Estelle had finished all the details of her newest scheme, then Sheila said, "I'll think about it."

"Do that. Sometimes you say that and I don't think you ever consider it again." She gathered her purse and stood.

"Leaving so soon?" Sheila asked as she ushered Estelle into the front of the house.

"I have a dozen things to do," Estelle complained happily.

"Marie, will you bring Mrs. Simon's coat?" Sheila asked as the maid appeared in the doorway. To Estelle she said, "Drive carefully. The streets are slippery."

That reminded Estelle of Mike Barlow. "Sheila," she said, "you know I look on you as a sister, and what I'm about to say is in your best interest."

Sheila suppressed a sigh. Suggestions phrased like that were always marginally offensive.

"Don't have anything to do with that Barlow boy. Believe me. I know what I'm talking about." She took her wrap from Marie without bothering to thank her.

"Goodbye, Estelle. Tell Ed hello for me."

When the woman left, Sheila closed the door thoughtfully. Estelle's warning not to see Mike again carried no weight at all. But the word "boy" did. Sheila went to the ornate cheval glass in the foyer and critically studied her face. No wrinkles; no gray hairs. But she was five years older than Mike. Did that matter?

George had been her senior by ten years. He had already been in his residency when she had entered college. That put him in a different generation from Mike. She added rapidly in her head. When she was thirteen, Mike was only eight. She could have been his baby-sitter! That brought a groan to her lips. The family feud was a minor thing, but her age could be a real drawback. Turning away, she went upstairs to soak in a bubble bath while she considered this new problem.

Mike stayed busy all that day. Not only had several more cars ended up in ditches, but the plows had buried the usual number under banks of snow and some of the owners needed assistance towing them out.

By late afternoon he was more than ready to call it a day. His pockets bulged with money, and his back ached. His house was in a much less prestigious section of town than Sheila's, where the trees weren't quite as tall or the streets quite as wide, and where children played in snowy yards to the accompaniment of barking dogs. Mike parked in his drive and waved to a group of neighborhood kids who were building a snowman next door. For a few minutes he watched their progress from his front porch as he fitted his key into the lock. He had always liked children and hoped to have some of his own someday.

Going inside, he stamped the snow off his feet on the throw rug in his entryway, then headed straight for the kitchen and flicked on the light. Following his usual procedure, Mike pulled off his boots and walked in his stocking feet to turn up the heater. The furnace roared to life, forcing warm air through the floor vents.

He took a pepperoni pizza out of the freezer and turned on the oven before going to his bedroom to hang up his coat. Sitting on his bed, he pulled on his sneakers and ran his fingers back and forth through his hair. The cap he wore was warm, but it had flattened his hair against his head.

Going back to the kitchen, he put the pizza in to bake, popped the top on a beer and sat on the countertop to wait. Out the window he saw his tiny wooden-fence-enclosed backyard. A clothesline left by the previous owners sagged in one corner of the yard. Mike had never used it for anything but drying his car mats whenever he cleaned the truck.

Looking around the kitchen, he noticed the walls and cabinets needed another scrubbing and possibly a fresh coat of paint. But the painting could be done later. His usual practice was to wait until repairs were actually needed before he tackled them, adhering to the premise that "if it works, don't fix it." While he waited, he absently ran his fingers over the square tiles of the countertop where he sat. Several were cracked, and no amount of elbow grease could lighten the aged grout between them.

He wasn't at all sure what Sheila's house looked like inside, but he was sure it was a far cry from this one. Despondently he leaned back against the cabinet door. They might get around the family problem between them—Sheila didn't act like a Danforth and that was good enough for him—but her money, that was another problem. Mike had more than his share of pride, and he wasn't about to have it said that he courted a woman for her money. Or that he was a gigolo.

Could he see her and not have her think he was after her bank account? What would their friends say? He was willing to bet that Sheila's sister-in-law had had plenty to say once he had left. Thank goodness he hadn't been stranded with *that* Danforth.

He braced his palms on the tiles beside him and swung down. Wandering into his living room, he knelt on the hearth and started a fire. Taking his guitar from its corner, he lounged on the recliner and picked out a melody as his eyes studied the flames and his mind recalled every detail of Sheila.

To even consider seeing her socially was foolish. She was as unattainable as the most fanciful of his dreams. By now she had probably decided that she had made a big mistake in being so friendly with him. She was probably laughing about him at that very minute. No, he told himself, Sheila wasn't that cruel, but she was, no doubt, regretting having been so open with him. Especially after that Estelle got through with her.

He recalled her exclamation on seeing Estelle. Those two didn't get along, he could tell. And no wonder. Two women couldn't be more opposite.

Absently Mike wondered why he thought he was such an expert on Sheila Danforth. They had been together only a few hours. Yet he seemed to know her as well as he knew friends of several years' standing. There was something between them. Something that wasn't new. It was as if they had known each other before. Had loved before.

His fingers stilled on the strings, and he gazed into the fire. Surely love didn't come like this—so suddenly and yet so familiarly between two strangers. Surely he didn't love her. She couldn't possibly love him.

The shrill ringing of the phone jarred him out of his reverie. "Hello?"

"Mike? This is Sheila. Am I disturbing you?"

He was so amazed to hear her voice that he hadn't heard what she asked. "What did you say?"

"I asked if I was disturbing you."

"No, no. I wasn't doing anything in particular." He leaned forward as if to get closer to her silken voice.

"I was calling about my car. Have you had a chance to look at it?"

"Not yet. I plan to see about it first thing tomorrow." How could a woman sound so sexy and just be talking about a car?

"There's no real rush. I was only wondering if you could deliver it when you're through. Say about six o'clock."

"Six?" he asked, thinking of how she looked when she tilted her head to gaze up at him. She was so delicate and feminine.

"Would another time be more convenient?"

"Six is fine." He shook his head and chided himself for being foolish. This was a business call. Nothing else.

"Great. And, Mike, since that's so near dinnertime, will you stay and eat with me?" There was an expectant pause as if she were holding her breath.

Mike grinned. "I guess I could do that, if you won't go to any trouble." That was stupid, he thought. The maid would cook it.

"No trouble at all. But be warned—it's my maid's day off and I'll be the cook. Want to change your mind?"

"No way, lady. I'll see you tomorrow night at six." Mike hung up the phone, a Cheshire cat grin splitting his face. Then the odor of a burning pizza got his attention, and he hurried to the kitchen to see if it was salvageable.

Chapter Four

You look particularly pleased with yourself today,"
Gail Taylor said as she drove with Sheila toward
Springfield. "Did you finally tell Estelle where to get
off?"

Sheila smiled at her best friend and shook her head.
"Estelle means well."

"Sure she does. Just like Lucrezia Borgia. If you
didn't get the best of Estelle, then why are you all
smiles?"

Trying unsuccessfully to wipe the smile off her face,
Sheila said evasively, "I hope the pianist is good, since
we're driving two whole hours to get there."

"He's good or he wouldn't be a concert pianist and
the Springfield Women's Forum wouldn't be honor-
ing him with a luncheon. But you're changing the
subject. What's going on with you?"

"I met somebody." Sheila smoothed the pleated skirt of her navy and white woolen suit.

"You did?" Gail was so amazed at Sheila's admission that she almost drove off the road. "I didn't know you had been out of town."

"I haven't."

"Then how could you meet anyone new? We already know all the men in Falls River. It's not that large a town."

"We haven't met quite all of them. Watch the road."

"Well?" Gail demanded eagerly. "Who is he?"

"His name is Mike Barlow."

"Say that again?"

"You heard me. Barlow."

"Are you trying to tell me you're seeing a Barlow?" Gail asked with a laugh. "That's great. Estelle must be having a fit."

"She is."

"Where did you meet him?"

Sheila hesitated. This was the tricky part. "I met him the night before last when my car ran off the road. It's still in the shop. That's why I asked you to drive today." She drew a deep breath. "Mike operates a tow truck, and he pulled me out of the ditch. The storm was so bad we had to stay overnight in a little cafe."

Gail was staring at Sheila whenever she could take her eyes off the road. "Did you say he drives a tow truck?"

"Yes, that's right."

"Let me see if I have this straight. You met a man named Mike Barlow the night before last, he drives a tow truck, and you're going out with him?"

"Not exactly going out with him. He's coming over for dinner tonight. It's Marie's night off, and I thought I'd make lasagna. Do you think I can make it without burning it this time? Maybe I should stick with spaghetti."

"Who cares about the menu? What I want to know is if you've lost your mind. You don't date someone just because he pulls you out of a ditch. Are you just doing this to irritate Estelle?"

"Of course not. You'd understand if you met him."

Realizing that this was no joke, Gail's tone switched from amusement to genuine interest. "What does he look like?"

"He's incredibly sexy. And handsome. His hair is a dark gold, and his eyes are just a shade darker. And he's tall."

"Why do the short women always meet the tall men?" Gail muttered. "Come on now—are you really going to date him?"

"I will if he asks me. I hope he does."

"A tow truck driver. And a Barlow." Gail's voice mirrored her disbelief. She wanted to be supportive of her best friend, but this seemed a bit outrageous.

"Gail, you're my best friend. If you don't understand, no one will."

"I'm trying, I'm trying. But this takes some getting used to."

"He also owns a garage." Sheila smiled contentedly. "His hobby is restoring vintage cars."

"A garage? You mean like a repair place?"

Sheila nodded. "My car is there now."

Gail grinned and shook her blond head. "I guess you know what you're doing, but it sounds crazy to me."

"You really would like him. He's so easy to talk to."

"You only met him the night before last. How do you know if you like him so well or not?"

"We were snowed in overnight together."

Gail raised her eyebrows. "Oh?"

"Nothing like that. We talked. And we danced. That's all."

"After all the matchmaking I've tried to do for you since George died, and you go out and find a garage mechanic. Maybe you're just lonely."

Sheila was silent for a minute. She had expected Gail to be more supportive. "I really am lonely, but that's not it," she finally answered. "There have been times I thought I'd bounce off the walls from loneliness in that monstrosity of a house. Why George wanted to live in a museum piece is still beyond me. But that's not why I want to see Mike."

"Are you sure it's not?"

"He isn't the only man who's asked me out," she reminded Gail. Technically he hadn't asked her out at all, she thought with a rush of insecurity. Maybe he wasn't at all interested in her. "Mike is different from any other man I've ever known."

"I'll buy that."

"No, I'm serious. There's something about him that sets him apart from all the rest. Please understand, Gail. I think I could care for him a great deal."

Now it was Gail's turn for silence. At last she said, "Be very careful, Sheila. He may not play by our rules. You could get hurt."

"You're absolutely right. I could. Because I'm not playing."

Sheila was unusually quiet during the rest of the drive and all through the luncheon. The musician was excellent, but Sheila's mind really wasn't on the music. Musicales weren't one of Sheila's major interests; she had primarily come with Gail to keep her company. Sheila's mind kept wandering to Mike. As much as she hated to admit it, Gail was the most liberal of her circle of friends. If her own best friend wouldn't be more understanding, how could she expect anyone else to be? This went beyond his being a Barlow. Gail was shocked at the way Mike earned his living. Sheila knew she shouldn't blame Gail. Up until the snowstorm, Sheila had never known a blue-collar worker, either. Yet Mike was different.

On the way home, Sheila was glad to talk about other subjects, and made no effort to swing the conversation back to Mike. Gail seemed to be avoiding the topic as well.

By the time she was deposited on her doorstep, Sheila was tired from not talking about the primary subject on her mind. She waved goodbye to Gail and let herself into the house.

Silence greeted her. Sheila had always hated being alone in this house. It was old and seemed to pop and creak in an eerie way when she was all by herself. The downstairs rooms were stiffly formal, thanks to George and his interior decorator. Most of the bedrooms were shut away in readiness for guests or children—whichever had happened to come first. Sheila was accustomed to sleeping alone, but she could never get used to the stillness of an empty house.

She went to the den and turned on the stereo to an easy-listening station, then increased the volume so it could be heard from almost anyplace in the house. She had never understood how to use the complicated intercom George had had installed. Even George had seldom used it.

Going upstairs, she hummed with the music—not because she felt like singing, but in order to hear a human voice. She wasn't afraid here, she reminded herself, just lonely. Besides, if ever there were a burglar in the house, she would rather him hear her and run away than for her to stumble quietly upon him.

Her bedroom was at the head of the stairs and across a wide hallway. Originally the room, with its full bath and small sitting room, had been occupied by the two of them as the master bedroom. But after a year and a half George had moved into the smaller one across the hall, saying that he didn't want to awaken her on those nights when he came home very late from the hospital. She wondered if George really thought she believed that excuse. She never let him know how hurt she had been when he had moved out of her room. He wouldn't have understood if she had. His parents had had separate rooms all his life, and so did Estelle and Ed. All the Danforths slept apart from their spouses, and preferred it that way.

Sheila undressed and hung her suit in the closet. "I've never fitted into this family," she said aloud. Talking to herself had become another of her new traits.

She studied the clothes hanging on the long rack and tried to decide what to wear for her dinner with Mike. She didn't want to dress up; that might look as if she were flaunting her money or trying to impress him. On the other hand, she didn't want him to think the occasion didn't warrant her wearing something special. She decided to put off the decision until later and wear a sweat suit until the meal was underway. She pulled on a fleecy knit pullover and drawstring pants in lemon yellow. Hopping on one foot, she put on white tennis shoes. Her hair kept falling in her eyes so she drew it back in a ponytail.

The kitchen was at the back of the house past the den and was Marie's special domain. Sheila always felt a little as though she were trespassing when she was there. The woodwork and countertop were gleaming white, and dark blue canisters matched the Italian tile floor.

Deciding she should make the dessert first, Sheila went to the walk-in pantry. Although Marie had a great disdain for mixes, she did keep the pantry stocked with a few things that Sheila wanted on hand for those times when she got the urge to cook on Marie's day off.

After digging through several cookbooks, she found a peach cobbler recipe under the heading of "jiffy dishes." She read it through and decided it wasn't too complicated for her to handle. This section of the book was unspotted and not dog-eared, meaning Marie always skipped over it. That was a good sign because Marie really enjoyed the challenge of the difficult dishes.

Marie had reorganized the kitchen again, so Sheila had some difficulty gathering the ingredients, a cooking dish and the measuring cups, but at last she had it all together. She appraised it. This wasn't a standard peach cobbler, but it did look interesting. She turned the oven on to preheat, remembering that she should have done that earlier. Why was the oven temperature always on the last line of the recipe anyway?

Not as confident as she had hoped she would be, Sheila had abandoned the idea of lasagna in favor of spaghetti. She filled a very large pot with water before lugging it over to the stove. She turned on the burner, then started searching for spaghetti. At last she found it and tore open the plastic wrapper with her teeth as she gauged the heat of the water. Small bubbles were forming around the outer edge of the pot so she decided it must be hot enough. Since she never knew quite how much spaghetti to cook in order to get the proper amount, she dumped the entire package in and turned away. Next she had to concoct a sauce.

She went back to the cookbook and turned hopefully to the jiffy section. The fluorescent lights caught the diamonds of her wedding rings, and Sheila paused. She had no reason to continue wearing them.

Slowly she pulled the set of rings off and held them up to the light where they sparkled and glittered. Their absence left a pale indentation on her ring finger, and her hand felt curiously free without their accustomed spacing.

Still gazing at the rings, Sheila went into the library and pulled out a group of false books. Behind it was the small wall safe where all her jewelry and important papers were kept. Closing the rings in her palm, Sheila dialed the safe's combination. She should have done this months ago. Pulling out a velvet-lined drawer, she dropped the rings in with several dinner rings and necklaces. When she closed the drawer and slammed the safe shut, Sheila felt an unexpected rush of freedom.

The melodious notes of the doorbell caused her to jump. Surely it wasn't that late! Replacing the false books in front of the safe, she hurried to answer the door.

Mike stood on her doorstep, his hands thrust in the pockets of his coat. Sheila stepped back and opened the door wide in greeting. "Are you early?" she asked.

"I don't think so." His easy amber gaze took in her flushed cheeks, ponytail, sweat suit and tennis shoes. She was even more beautiful than he remembered.

"Come in, come in. You must be freezing out there."

Mike stepped into the entry and looked around. The floor was white and looked as if it might be real marble. A curving staircase swept up an ivory and brocaded satin wall, and the chandelier was made up of hundreds of crystal prisms. Beyond the stairs he saw a formal living room that looked like a layout for an interior decorating magazine. He felt more than a little out of place.

"Let me take your coat." Sheila took it from him and hung it in a coat closet.

As she closed the closet door, their eyes met, and she slowed to a stop. Mike felt that unsettling sensation he had experienced in the cafe. Time seemed to have no meaning. Only the two of them existed.

"Is something burning?" he asked, to break the spell. A man could drown in those sea-green eyes and never mind at all.

"Burning!" Sheila ran toward the back of the house. As she passed the entry's gilt-framed mirror, she got a good look at herself in her flour-smudged sweat suit and her ponytail. "Oh, no!" she groaned, pulling the rubber band off her hair as she ran.

The pot of water was boiling in earnest, and a froth of starchy foam was dribbling down the side and onto the burner, sending up malodorous clouds of steam. Sheila turned off the knob and looked into the pot.

Mike peered curiously over her shoulder at the gelatinous oblong mass in the bottom of the pot. "What is it?"

"Spaghetti," she moaned. "I guess the water wasn't hot enough when I put it in."

"Is something in the oven?"

"Not yet," she said absently as she shoved the makeshift peach cobbler into the oven's depths. "Now there is."

Not wanting to ask what the dish was that she had put in the oven, Mike took a long spoon and poked at the mass of pasta at the bottom of the large pot. "I think it's a goner."

"Marie won't be happy about this. I think it's welded itself to the pot."

Mike pushed up the sleeves of his fisherman's knit sweater and searched for hot pads. "In a kitchen this size there's bound to be more food. We'll cook something else. I'll help you."

Sheila looked mournfully at the pot. "You'll never believe this, but I was trying to impress you. Favorably, that is."

He poured the mistake into the sink, ran the garbage disposal and ran more water in the pot to let it soak before he turned back to her. "Were you really? Trying to impress me, I mean."

"Yes, I really was." She ran her fingers through her hair and shoved it away from her face. "I know you have a low opinion of Danforths, and I wanted to change your mind. I was going to change clothes and freshen my makeup and dazzle you with my spaghetti." She smiled wryly. "I won't blame you if you'd rather leave."

He studied her as he tried to remember if anyone had ever tried to impress him before now. "I didn't come here just to eat. I'm here mainly to see you."

"Mainly?"

"And partly to see if I recalled you wrong. I did." When her face fell, he added, "You're a lot prettier than I remembered. And I notice you're no longer wearing your wedding rings."

Sheila glanced down at the pale line on her finger.

Before she could think of an answer, he said briskly, "Let's find something to eat. Can you scare up some cheese? I make an omelet like you won't believe."

After they ate, Mike surprised her further by insisting that he help her wash up. When the last dish was put away, they went into the den, and Sheila quickly turned the music down to a comfortable level. Mike pretended he saw nothing unusual with her elaborate stereo.

She sat on the couch, and he joined her. Mike was the first to break the awkward silence. "This room needs a fireplace."

"Originally there was one, but George disliked fireplaces so he had it paneled over. It's on that wall there behind the whatnot shelves."

"What about you? Did you want it boarded up?"

"I wasn't consulted. The decorator did everything George wanted. If it had been up to me, I would have left it open. I've always liked to sit by a fire. But I guess they are messy and drafty."

"A woman ought to have some say about her own house."

"I was young and impressionable at the time and didn't trust my tastes. It all happened at the time when I was still trying to fit into the family and not make waves."

"I get the feeling you make waves on a regular basis."

"These days I do. All my life I've had to fit into a mold of someone else's choosing. First my parents', then George's. Now I just want to be *me*."

Mike moved closer and studied her profile as she frowned at the place where the fireplace should have been. "If you were you, who would you be?"

She smiled and shook her head. "That's what frightens me. I'm not sure. But I'm narrowing down the sort of person I wouldn't be. I wouldn't belong to a club just because it's the 'right' one. And I wouldn't invite people to parties if I didn't like them, or go to theirs just because they invited me."

"Anything else?"

"I'd sell this house." She looked critically around the room. Even with two people in it, the house's silence seemed to be lying in wait.

Mike put his arm along the back of the couch and stroked her hair. It was every bit as soft and thick as he had expected. Sheila sat very still as if she was afraid he would stop if she moved. "Most people would give their right arm for a house like this," he said gently.

"Most people don't have to live in it." Her voice was scarcely more than a whisper. Grasping for something to say, she asked, "How was your day?"

"Busy. How was yours?" His deep voice was like a caress that reached her soul.

"About like it usually is. I went to a luncheon in Springfield with Gail. She's a very good friend. Maybe you could meet her sometime. The luncheon was in honor of a classical pianist. He played very well, but unfortunately I don't like classical music and . . ."

"Am I frightening you? You're shaking." His fingers stilled on her hair.

"No," she whispered. "I'm scaring myself."

She gazed into the gold-flecked depths of his eyes, feeling almost no separateness between herself and Mike. She knew she should move away or say something to break the mood, but that was the last thing she wanted.

"What are you afraid of?"

"I don't want to get hurt. I've kept everyone at a distance because I don't want to care, to fall in love again. Now I've met you and I'm confused."

His fingers smoothed the tender skin on her neck with a touch of gentle fire. "Love is nothing to be afraid of."

"Sometimes I think I don't even know what it is. It's supposed to grow between two people—to take time. I think I loved George, at least I thought so at the time. We were engaged for ages."

"Your marriage wasn't happy?"

"No. If he had lived, we would have divorced." She jerked her head up in surprise. "I never admitted that to anyone! How do you do that? Get under my defenses, I mean." She moved away and stared at him warily.

"I didn't mean to make you tell me more than you wanted to."

"You didn't make me do it. You made me *want* to."

"Maybe it's because you know you can trust me."

"Can I, Mike?" she asked with great reservation. "Can I really trust you?"

Before answering, he leaned forward and rested his forearms on his legs. "I don't know what's going on between us. We ought to be strangers and here we are talking about love and trust. You're pretty damned scary yourself."

"You don't talk about these things to just everybody, then?"

"I never talk about these things to anybody at all."

"Maybe," she said in a shaken voice, "maybe we ought to back off. Not see each other."

"I came over here all primed to tell you just that. Then you answered the door in that yellow outfit with flour on the front and your hair in a ponytail, and it started all over again."

"What did?"

"I'm not sure, but I'm having a hell of a time fighting it."

"Maybe it's just a physical thing," she managed to say. "You know, one of those biological urges."

"Lust at first sight? No way. I've been in lust, and this is something entirely different." He stood abruptly. "Look, I've said way too much. I think I'd better go."

Sheila slowly got to her feet as he crossed to the door. "Don't go," she said softly.

He paused and turned. The air between them was charged with an emotion that pulled them together. After what seemed like forever, he said, "Are you sure you know what you're saying?"

She crossed to him and gazed up searchingly. "Don't leave me."

Mike put his arms around her and drew her into his embrace. Lowering his head, he kissed her, gently at first, then more deeply as her velvety lips parted beneath his. Her hands slid up the hard muscles of his arms, meeting behind his neck. She arched her body against his as if she could become one with him.

Shaken, Mike drew back. "Lady, I think we're starting something we may not ever finish."

Sheila knew she should pull away, but for the first time in her life she had an overwhelming sense of rightness. Of belonging. Silently she took his hand and led him through the house to the stairs.

At the bottom Mike paused and looked up before meeting her searching gaze. "If either of us had any sense, we'd run in the opposite direction."

"Do you want to run? Mike, I'm not asking for more than you want to give. I'm not looking for a commitment. And I don't want you to think I make a habit of doing this." Her green gaze faltered. "The truth is, no man has been in this house in a year. Until I met you I thought I had all those switches turned off, permanently."

"Sheila," he said softly.

"I'm not the kind of woman who gives herself to just anybody. What I feel for you is more than I can turn my back on. If it lasts one night or if it lasts a week, at least I will have had that time."

"If I thought it wouldn't last more than a night, I wouldn't go up those stairs," Mike told her. "As for anything lasting, who knows? There are never any guarantees. We aren't two teenagers out for a thrill. In a way that makes it more frightening. I'm afraid if we go upstairs we won't ever be the same."

Sheila waited for Mike to decide. She knew in her heart that what he stirred in her was far more than anything covered in a biology book. She wanted him to be sure.

"On the other hand," he said as he caressed the curve of her cheek, "we might be much better than we were before." Putting his arm around her, they went upstairs.

In her bedroom, Mike turned off the overhead light, leaving a lamp burning on the dresser. The shade cast a rosy glow over the room, making it seem even cozier. He ran his fingers through the night shadows of her hair and tilted her face back to meet his lips.

Sheila had never been kissed with such expertise, and she felt her pulse leap with desire. Having been this bold, she couldn't quite bring herself to make the next move. She was in an agony between wanting Mike and being worried over what he might think of her attempts at seduction.

"Hey," he said softly. "Where did you go?"

"I don't want you to think I'm a loose woman," she answered in a small voice.

"Honey, that's the last thing I would think," he reassured her. "I think you're warm, desirable, sexy, intriguing . . . but never loose."

She smiled tremulously and looked up into his face.

"I also think you're short," he said as he grinned down at her. "If we do much of this I'm going to have to get you a step stool."

Sheila laughed and he hugged her close so that she could hear the muffled thud of his heart. Experimentally she ran her hand under his sweater and felt the firm warmth of his back. "You feel good," she murmured. It had been so long since a man had held her and kissed her. So very long.

Mike eased her sweatshirt over her head and tossed it onto the nearby chair. She was gracefully slender, and her bra was no more than a scrap of lace. He could tell by her eyes that she was a little afraid, and he smiled at her encouragingly as he released the hooks that held her bra and pulled it away. Her soft, firm flesh enticed him, and he knew he would never turn away.

A blush colored Sheila's cheeks as he gazed at her. She suddenly felt very inadequate. What if she wasn't good enough?

Mike pulled off his sweater and dropped it on the carpet. Sheila's eyes widened as she admired him. She hadn't expected him to be so well-built. He was a mechanic, not an athlete.

"Kick off your shoes," he prodded. When she complied, he untied the drawstring that held up her pants.

Her bikini panties were as lacy as her bra had been and were as easily removed. Hungrily Mike let his eyes feast on the luscious curves of her body. Her breasts weren't large, but they were more generous than he had expected. Her waist tapered to slenderness and curved lower into her hips. She wasn't thin, but there wasn't an extra ounce of flesh anywhere except in the right places. Her legs were smooth and well-shaped, and her feet were small. She was as perfect as anyone could be.

Sheila waited nervously as he perused her. Her breasts were too small, and she knew she weighed five pounds too much. What would he think of her? She didn't remember being this nervous on her wedding night.

"You're so beautiful," he murmured, reaching out to touch the pouting bud of one breast. "I never expected you to be so perfect."

He seemed to mean what he said, and a wave of relief washed over her. "You're perfect, too," she ventured. Lifting her hand, she ran her fingertips over the hard wall of his chest and over the lean ridges of his belly. The smooth copper skin thrilled her.

Their eyes met, and again she felt her senses swirl. Then he kissed her, and she felt her taut nipples graze his chest before he caught her to him.

Barely taking time to pull back the covers, Mike placed her on the bed and removed the rest of his clothes as he gazed down at her. Framed on the pale blue sheets, she looked like his image of Venus, and he ached with longing for her. He watched her eyes travel over his naked body, and he took a deep breath, forcing himself to give her time to finish her survey before he lowered himself onto the bed.

Bending over her, he trailed warm, moist kisses from her ear down to her shoulder. Then he moved to her breasts, taking one eager nipple into his mouth and teasing it until she trembled with pleasure. His hot tongue and muffled whispers urged her to greater desire, and she arched against him, her hands exploring the planes and undulations of his body. Moving to the other breast, Mike slipped his arm under her to lift her toward his hungry lips. He was trembling from his need of her, and as his hand strayed lower to seek out her femininity, an answering tremor coursed through her.

Sheila opened herself to his fingers, and when he found the treasure he sought, she sighed his name. With relentless tenderness he brought her desire to a flaming crescendo. Just when she thought she could bear it no more, he positioned himself over her and entered her, filling her, making her feel wholly his. She gasped as his sensuous movements sent her senses and soul reeling beyond her greatest expectations. Her world seemed about to explode with the intensity of her pleasure, and she held him tightly, breathlessly repeating his name. She cried out as ecstasy engulfed her, seeming to cascade over her and sweep her away in an uncontrollable tide.

Gradually her world settled back into place, her awareness of it slowly returning. As her breathing quieted, she realized that, before this, if anyone had asked her if she had ever been sexually satisfied, she would have said yes. But now she knew she had never even suspected such fulfillment was possible. Sleepily she started to tell Mike so, but before the words could form, he surprised her by again moving deep within her.

Her amazement quickly turned to pleasure, and much to her surprise, she felt her body responding and the rapture building again. This time when she reached the peak of her desire, he soared with her, and she cried out in sheer ecstasy.

Still in each other's arms, they cuddled and murmured words of contentment as their satisfied bodies mellowed into sleep.

Chapter Five

Mike woke at dawn as was his usual practice. For a few minutes he blinked up at the unfamiliar ceiling, trying to recall what had been dream and what reality. His eyes lowered to the lilac-and-white wallpaper and the ruffled eyelet curtains that surrounded the window, and he jerked his head to look at the other side. That had been no dream.

Sheila lay fast asleep, her slender body curled against the warmth of his side. Her dark hair fanned over the pale blue pillow case. Only her curving eyebrows and her closed eyes were visible beneath the lavender blanket and white spread.

Moving slowly so as not to awaken her, Mike pulled the covers lower so he could see the rest of her face. She was smiling slightly as if she were in the midst of a pleasant dream. Her eyelashes made a lacy fringe against the cream of her cheek, and her dewy lips were sensually enticing. One of her hands lay on the pillow, her fingers curling like delicate petals. A slow pulse beat steadily in the hollow of her throat. That she had shared herself with him was almost miraculous.

Easing himself out of bed, he dressed quietly, never taking his eyes off her. When her hand strayed to his pillow as if in search of him, he smiled. They had been good for each other. No one could deny that. She had filled a void he had ignored for a long time. Even with her halfway across the room, he felt as if they were still one.

He wanted to kiss her goodbye, but he was reluctant to disturb her sleep. Instead, he lovingly gazed at her for a brief time, trying to memorize the curve of her cheek and the highlights in her hair. Last night had been perfect, but he didn't delude himself that it might ever happen again. Although what he felt for her was much more than a passing fancy, he knew they were from different worlds. Whatever they felt for each other, they couldn't hope to break free and make a world of their own.

He sighed and turned away. What made him think, even for a minute, that Sheila would want to change her world for him? Chiding himself for being a hopeless dreamer, he went downstairs and left.

As he headed down Sheila's driveway on foot, planning to walk to work in hopes that the crisp air and vigorous exercise might help clear his mind of his unattainable fantasies, the biting cold of early dawn sent shivers through him. It was much colder than he had expected. After turning up the collar of his heavy coat, he fished in his pocket and found the keys to the Mercedes. Thankful that he had forgotten to give them to her the night before, Mike climbed into the glove-leather seat and pulled the door closed against the biting cold.

As he drove through the quiet streets, he decided that when Carl, his younger cousin who worked for him, came to work, the two of them should deliver Sheila's car. No one would know he had been there all night. Mike felt a unique sense of responsibility to protect Sheila.

At eight o'clock Carl showed up for work, his tow-head still tousled from sleep. Mike was already busy, his cheerful whistle echoing against the cool cement of the bay. He grinned and called a greeting to the teen-ager. The boy nodded and waved halfheartedly as he stumbled toward the coffeepot. Carl had always been a slow starter on cold mornings. Or on warm ones, for that matter, but he knew his way around an engine and was willing to work for minimum wage.

Mike slammed the hood of the Ford he had been repairing. It could wait. He wanted to deliver Sheila's car before she needed it. As he washed up, he called out to his cousin. "Hey, Carl. Follow me over to 12 Hazelglen. I need to deliver the Danforth car."

Carl made a motion that meant he heard and understood. Mike put on his coat and pulled his wool cap over his ears. He couldn't get the image of Sheila out of his mind. The thought of her beautiful smile, the way she tilted her head as she talked, the way she had cried out with pleasure in the dark of the night. When Mike realized he was smiling, he turned away so Carl wouldn't notice.

Next door to the garage was Mabel Koepke's small flower shop. Climbing over drifts of snow, Mike knocked on the back door.

"We aren't open for business yet," the woman began as she was opening the service door. "Oh, it's you, Mike. I'm not open yet, you know."

"I know. That's why I came around back. I need a rose."

"You need a rose?" She stared at him in disbelief, her gray eyebrows arching. "Now why would anybody need a rose this early in the morning?"

He grinned winningly. "A red one. Come on, Mrs. Koepke. Do me a favor and let me buy one. I can't wait for you to open."

"Mabel. Please. Mrs. Koepke is my mother-in-law. How many times should I have to tell you this?"

Mike could easily see through the woman's mock seriousness. "Okay, Mabel. Now, how about the rose?"

"So are you going to just stand out there in the cold until you catch your death?" The woman gestured for him to come in. "You want a rose? So I'll get you a rose. Heaven forbid you should learn patience."

Mike fished money out of his pocket as Mabel took a perfectly formed red rose out of the refrigerated display case. She tied a red bow on the stem and stapled a gift card to the ribbon.

"I never knew you to need a rose, Mike. Got a special girl, maybe?"

"Maybe." His grin widened as he paid for the flower. "Thanks...Mabel." Mike winked at the older woman.

"Tell her she's a lucky girl," she called after him. "You're a nice boy."

Mike laughed. To Mabel Koepke he would always be a boy.

He got in the Mercedes and drove through the awakening streets. Falls River was preparing for another day. Mike looked longingly at the bare trees; the branches met and laced over the quiet streets. He was ready for spring. Especially now.

He parked the car under the portico and took a pen from his shirt pocket. He wanted to write something on the card, but he wasn't sure what. There was so much he wanted to say, and he was half-afraid to say any of it. He didn't really know how she felt about him.

After an agonizing few moments, Mike wrote, "Thanks for the memory." That wasn't exactly what he wanted to say, but it would have to do. He knew for a fact the memory of last night would never leave him.

Carl drove up in the truck, and Mike poked the Mercedes's keys through the mail slot in the front door and left.

Sheila slept later than was her custom. Only the persistent ringing of the doorbell aroused her. Sleepily she looked at the clock. Nine o'clock. She turned toward the empty side of the bed. The pillow still held the imprint of Mike's head, but the sheets were cold to her touch. With a sigh she realized he must have left without waking her. Although it was very thoughtful of him, she wished he hadn't. She had so much she wanted to say to him. Things she couldn't possibly say other than with a kiss.

When the doorbell rang again, Sheila got out of bed and slipped on her green velvet robe. She couldn't recall ever having slept naked, and the thought made her smile. It was wonderful to have had a reason to wake up naked.

Hoping Mike might have come back after something, Sheila ran down the stairs and through the house to the side door. As she flung the door open, her smile faded. It was only Estelle.

"Were you still in bed?" Estelle asked in surprise. "I thought you always got up early."

"I guess I slept late. What are you doing with that rose?"

Estelle handed it to her. "I found it on the front seat of your car. Why would there be a rose in there?"

A gentle smile curved Sheila's lips as she inhaled the rose's rich aroma. She didn't need to read the card to know who had brought it.

"Aren't you going to answer me? The card says something about a memory."

"You read the card? Estelle!"

"I could hardly help it. There's no envelope." Estelle took off her fur coat and tossed it over the back of a chair.

"Maybe I have a secret admirer," Sheila hedged, her Mona Lisa smile still intact.

"You'd better be careful, is all I have to say. There are a lot of nuts running loose in the world."

Sheila ignored her as she put the flower in a crystal bud vase. Just looking at it brought back memories of the night before and of how Mike had held her and made love with her. Sheila's smile broadened, and she turned her head so Estelle wouldn't see.

"I do hope you aren't getting involved with some-one again so soon," Estelle said peevishly. "Isn't there any coffee made?"

"I just got up and Marie isn't here yet."

"She gets later all the time."

"No, she doesn't. One of her children has a cold, and I told her she could come in later." Sheila sat in a chair opposite Estelle and curled her feet beneath her. "What if I am seeing someone? Surely you knew I would in time, and it has been quite a while."

"I suppose you must eventually," Estelle admit-ted. "You're still young. It's just that it seems like yesterday that you and George were newlyweds and so very happy."

"That was a long time ago," Sheila reminded her gently. "I know you miss George, but life goes on. I don't want to be alone forever."

Estelle looked around the elegant morning room. "I suppose not. It's just so hard to believe George won't ever be here again. I remember when you bought these chairs. George was so happy to have this house and to be on his own at last. He stayed home longer than most sons would have. But then Mother was so feeble toward the end." Estelle sighed again. "I did all I could for her, but George was always able to manage her better than I could. He reminded her so much of Father, you know."

"Yes, so I was told."

Estelle ran her hand over the polished chintz of the upholstered chair. "You should have known George as a boy. We all knew he would make a mark on the world. I remember how he always used to say to me,

'Estelle, someday I'm going to do something everyone will remember.' He was like that.''

Sheila tried to look sympathetic. Estelle's regrets over George's untimely death were quite real, but Sheila had heard it all many times, and this morning she wanted to look forward, not back. All her thoughts were for Mike.

"I suppose you're wondering why I came by so early," Estelle said, leaning forward as if to include Sheila in a confidence. "I was on my way to Ed's law office to have him draw up those papers we discussed."

"Papers?"

"The George P. Danforth Cardiovascular Research Foundation." Estelle made the words sound as if they were emblazoned in forty-foot-tall neon lights. With misty eyes, she looked earnestly at Sheila. "It's the mark George meant to make. The mark he would have made if only he'd had the chance."

Vague memories of Estelle's new scheme to get control of George's money came back to Sheila; she hadn't paid much attention at the time. "A research foundation?"

"Isn't it a perfectly marvelous inspiration? Doctors from all over the world can benefit from it, and it will all be in George's name."

"I don't understand. Are you talking about funds for research?"

"Of course. We talked about it just the other day. Surely you can't have forgotten." Estelle drew back to show her displeasure with Sheila's forgetfulness. "How could you not remember something so important?"

"Who would head this foundation? How does it work?"

"I have volunteered to act as head because I know you don't like dealing with such technical decisions. It will be a tremendous undertaking, but I'll make the time. It's my contribution to George's memory. Naturally you will be on the board of directors," she added hastily, "along with a number of notable doctors in the cardiovascular field. A sum will be set aside to fund the foundation, and doctors will apply to us for grants. Think of the good we can accomplish."

"What sum did you have in mind?"

"Well," Estelle evaded, "George was a very wealthy man. The Danforth money is almost legendary around here. As you know, Mother left virtually all of it to George for some reason—I think her mind wandered a bit toward the end. Not that I ever resented it. It was her money, and George was the perfect son." In spite of her benevolent words, Estelle's expression grew bitter.

"Ed is rich, too," Sheila reminded her. "You have never wanted for anything."

"What an idea," Estelle said as she laughed brittlely. "As if a woman in my position were *needy*. My goodness, Sheila, you have such a strange way of putting things."

Sheila drew back. Estelle didn't allow anyone to get close to her, and she always rejected any intimation of affection. In her own way Estelle was lonely, too, but Estelle was determined to stay that way.

"Now, about this research foundation. Can't you see how this is something we simply must do? It's the perfect memorial for George."

"Estelle, try to understand this. I don't want to give away all my money. I enjoy living the good life just as you do. I don't want to give it up. As for George, we were never very happy together as you well know."

"The very idea! I know nothing of the kind! George was an ideal husband."

Sheila remembered all the nights her "ideal" husband had come in smelling of some other woman's perfume, and how often she had had to maneuver his drunken steps toward his bed. There were seldom harsh words between them because there were seldom any words at all. The last time she had objected to his excessive drinking, he had struck her and knocked her down. Sheila didn't consider this to be an ideal marriage. Abruptly she stood up. "I'll think about it, Estelle. I really will. But don't have Ed draw up the papers just yet. I like the idea of a research foundation, but not for all the money. Perhaps for a portion."

"But you have your own money, and what George left you is Danforth money!"

"And I'm a Danforth," Sheila pointed out.

"No! You will never be a real Danforth," Estelle ground out, all her pretense at gentility gone. Having uttered the worst condemnation she could think of, Estelle grabbed her coat and left in a huff.

Sheila shook her head in disbelief as the door slammed behind her sister-in-law. Estelle was impossible to like, but Sheila couldn't help feeling sorry for her.

Going back upstairs, Sheila ran the bathwater in her large rose-marble Roman tub. Normally she preferred to shower, but for thinking she had never found anything more conducive than a bubble bath. Pouring in a liberal amount of bath crystals, Sheila watched the bubbles foam up.

When the tub was full, she hung her robe on the brass hook and stepped into the tub. The hot water made her skin blush and tingle, and she sank down until her head rested on the tub's rim. As the bubbles tickled her skin and a fog of steam drifted upward, she at last let herself think about Mike.

Had last night meant as much to him as it had to her? Had it meant anything at all?

Sinking lower into the bubbles, Sheila wondered what Mike thought of her. In the light of day she was somewhat embarrassed to recall that she had been the aggressor. All the tasteless jokes she had ever heard about an older woman and a younger man taunted her. Had she made a fool of herself? In her marriage, Sheila had usually been the one to initiate sex because George's libido was so low. Last night she hadn't even questioned the role. Today she was growing more and more concerned that she had come on too strong. Still, Mike hadn't objected. And once they had reached the bedroom, he had been as eager as she had.

Sheila closed her eyes and tried to convince herself that she had not been too pushy. After all, he had sent her a rose. "Thanks for the memory." Did that mean he wouldn't be seeing her again? There was no reason to thank her for a memory if he intended to make other memories later.

She lifted her foot out of the water and idly ran her toes over the polished brass spigot. Soap suds glided down her silken leg to drip into the water. She wished she'd had more experience with men, or at least had someone she could go to for advice.

For a few moments she toyed with the notion of asking Gail's opinion. Gail was divorced and presumably had a love life. At least she dated frequently. But Sheila remembered how uncomfortable Gail had acted when she had heard what Mike did for a living. Sheila had never considered that her best friend might be a snob. Whether that was the reason for Gail's reaction or not, Sheila wouldn't feel right about asking Gail's advice on so personal a subject. And no one else could even be considered.

Sheila soaked in the tub, vacillating between wanting to see Mike and being afraid she had chased him off. The bubbles dissolved and the water grew tepid as she struggled over what she should do.

Never having been one to wallow in indecision, Sheila got out of the tub, dried off and put on what little makeup she wore. Then she dressed in dark gray pants, a striped silk blouse of red, blue and silver and a red sweater vest. After pulling on gray suede boots, Sheila slipped a long chain that gleamed like molten silver about her neck. She brushed her hair until it lay in soft brown skeins about her face.

As she left the house, she put on her fur parka and lifted the hood over her head. The sun was out, but the day was colder than when it had been cloudy.

Falls River wasn't a big town, so she had no trouble finding Barlow's Garage. Getting up the nerve to stop in front took a little more effort. On her third trip around the block, Sheila realized this looked pretty strange in itself, so she pulled into the small parking area. A boy with rumpled hair came out to meet her.

"Is Mr. Barlow here?" Sheila asked in a burst of courage.

"He's in the bay."

"Could I speak with him?"

"Sure. Go through the office."

Feeling very self-conscious, Sheila went through the doorway the boy had indicated and found herself in the large room where the repairs were done. At first she didn't see anyone, but the metallic ring of a tool pounding metal and then dropping onto concrete encouraged her to walk in.

Again the banging resumed. Sheila made her way between cars and saw a pair of legs sticking out from under a late-model car. "Mike?" she asked doubtfully.

At once the pounding stopped, and he slid out from under the car to stare up at her.

Suddenly Sheila realized she had been the aggressor again, and she blushed. Now he really would think she was chasing him. "Thanks for the rose," she murmured as she turned to beat a quick retreat.

"Wait a minute." Mike hurriedly got up, sending the creeper he'd been lying on rolling back under the car. As he wiped his hands on a rag, he called after her. "Don't rush off."

She turned to him, the anguish she was feeling showing clearly on her face. "Don't you see? I've done it again!"

Mike, who had no idea what she was talking about, tossed the rag down and stepped closer. "What are you talking about?"

"Oh, Mike, I feel just awful about this."

A muscle tightened on the ridge of his jaw. He was afraid she would regret having let him make love with her. "Oh?"

"I was feeling so guilty, and I came out here to tell you so, and now you must think I'm doing it again."

"I don't—"

"I know, I know. You must think I'm the pushiest person you've ever met. Just forget I ever came out here. No, you can't do that, can you? Well, I don't mean it the way it looks. You'll just have to take my word for it. But I didn't know if you would ever call me or not and I wanted to tell you I appreciate it. The rose, I mean. Oh, it's a lovely rose and so sweet of you. No, I don't mean sweet. And nice is such a tacky little word. It was good of you to—"

"Hold it," he interrupted. "I don't have any idea what you're talking about. Are you saying you're sorry about last night? If so, I can—"

"Sorry! Of course not! Why on earth would I be sorry about that?" She gazed up at him incredulously. "You're the one who doesn't want to come back."

"Where did you get that idea?" he demanded.

"Well, the card said, 'Thanks for the memory.' Doesn't that mean you don't want to see me again? What else could it mean? I know it's because I was too aggressive, and I can see why you were put off by that, but—"

"Hold it again. I wasn't put off."

"You weren't?"

"Did I act put off?" he asked in exasperation.

"You didn't mind that I was so aggressive? I mean if I hadn't been, we would never have . . ."

"Yes, we would have." Mike glanced around to be sure that Carl was not in earshot.

She smiled, and her face lit up. "We would?"

"And you weren't aggressive, just assertive." He grinned down at her. "I liked it. Look, the rules have changed about a woman having to pretend to be a vestal virgin until the man seduces her. We're equals. At least in that respect," he finished lamely. How could he claim equality with someone who wore the equivalent of his yearly income on her back?

"I like that," she surprised him by saying. "I've really been worrying over what you thought."

"Over what *I* thought? I've been worrying over what you must think of me." He lowered his voice. "A Barlow doesn't make love to a Danforth without repercussions."

"You made love *with* me, not *to* me. What repercussions?" she demanded in a stage whisper.

"How can you stand there wrapped in mink in my second-rate garage and ask me that?" His voice rose to match his mood.

So did hers. "This isn't mink, it's fox, and you're the biggest snob I ever met! No, wait. It's reverse snobbery, and that's even worse."

They glared at each other, neither willing to give an inch. When he couldn't stare her down, Mike said, "I should have known better than to get mixed up with a Danforth."

"There you go again! Can't we have a simple discussion without bringing George's family into it? Honestly," she raved, "I'm fed up to the teeth with hearing about George!"

"Well, why don't you buy some earplugs? You can afford them!"

"I knew I shouldn't have come out here! You may say you don't resent my being pushy, but you do!"

"All I resent is being told what I think! You don't know what I think at all. You don't even know who I am!"

"Yes, I do! I know you better than you know yourself and you're just being pigheaded!"

"Pigheaded!"

"You heard me!" She stormed away, leaving him glaring after her. "Thanks again for the rose!" she yelled back at him. "Are you going to see me again or not?"

"If I had the sense God gave a goose, I'd never see you again, even if I had to move to China!" he retorted loudly.

"That doesn't answer my question." She frowned back at him.

"No!"

"I don't believe you!"

"One of us has to have some sense about this!" he roared.

"Here's my number." She pulled a card from her purse and stuck it on the bulletin board beside the door. The board shook from the assault, and the other notes and receipts jiggled. "It's unlisted, so don't lose it!"

"I should have left you in the snow!" he affirmed as she slammed out.

Sheila smiled. He might sound gruff, but she had a feeling he didn't mean it. And he looked incredibly virile standing there in his work clothes. She was still smiling when she drove off.

Mike glared after her, but he wasn't really mad. He just couldn't figure her out; it was so damned exasperating. Going to the bulletin board, he used his pocketknife to dig out the thumbtack she had embedded in the cork. Glancing at the number on the crisp white card, Mike smiled and slipped it into his pocket.

Chapter Six

I just love this tearoom,'' Estelle purred contentedly.

Sheila glanced around at the profusion of ferns and ivies that tastefully decorated the room. Beautiful stained glass window hangings strategically blocked the view of the parking lot where the sun had begun to melt the snow. The August Teahouse had become a favorite luncheon spot for their crowd after a morning of shopping. She sipped her rose hip tea and nodded. "It's nice here."

Gail noted, "There aren't many people here today."

"No, they're probably all still in the casual-wear department of Millard's. Have you ever seen such a crowd?" Estelle ground out her cigarette and sent a stream of smoke upward from her pursed lips.

"It was packed," Gail agreed. "That's an adorable silk dress you bought. It will be perfect with your patent leather heels—the ones with tiny black straps."

Sheila studied the rosy hue of her tea and wondered what Mike was doing. She had wanted to stay home today, in case he called, but she had already promised to go shopping with Gail and Estelle. They went out together once a week, and at one time Sheila had looked forward to their outings. Now she only wanted to be alone with her thoughts. There was so much she needed to sort out, so many emotions she needed to examine.

Estelle was watching her critically. "You ought to get out more often. You look pale."

"I'm pale because it's wintertime," Sheila replied.

"What makes you think she isn't getting out?" Gail asked.

"What do you mean?" Estelle's pale eyes met Gail's.

Gail glanced at her friend and faltered as she answered, "I assumed you knew."

"Knew what?"

"Estelle, are you going to the charity benefit next week?" Sheila asked.

"Yes." To Gail she repeated her question. "Knew what?"

"That Sheila has been seeing someone." Gail looked helplessly at Sheila.

"Oh? Who is he?"

"I don't think I'll go to the benefit. Those things can be so boring. I'll just send a check instead," Sheila continued, hoping Estelle would take the hint.

Estelle leaned nearer. "Who are you dating? Is it Howard Bennington? I hope not. He's been divorced three times."

"It's not Howard," Gail murmured.

Sheila glared at her.

"Surely it's not Jamison Harris! He's old enough to be your father."

"Wrong again," Gail replied.

"Well, who's left? There simply aren't that many single men around here. Don't tell me it's Mareen Rosco's ex, what's his name!"

"I'm seeing Mike Barlow," Sheila blurted out. Estelle's reaction was as Sheila predicted.

First Estelle paled, then she became flushed with barely suppressed emotion. "Mike Barlow!"

"I'm sorry, Sheila," Gail said contritely. "I really thought Estelle knew."

"What is there to apologize for?" Sheila asked with a nervous laugh. "I'm single and so is he. Why shouldn't we see each other?"

"You're actually dating a *Barlow*? A garage mechanic?"

"You make it sound illegal. Really, Estelle, he's a very nice man."

"He's entirely unsuitable. I demand that you stop seeing him at once!"

"Demand?" Sheila asked in disbelief. "You have no right to tell me who I may or may not see."

"As head of the family I have every right!"

"No, you don't. In the first place we aren't medieval aristocracy, and in the second I don't consider you the head of the family. I was married to your brother. That's all. The family ties dissolved with his death."

"You'll lower our standing in this town being seen with this man. You're still a Danforth!"

"Make up your mind, Estelle. The last time we saw each other you assured me I would never be one."

Estelle glared at Sheila, her face as chalky and stiff as a mask. Gail moved uneasily and motioned for the waitress to bring the check.

Sheila put her money on the table to pay for her lunch, then stood. "I think I had better leave. I'll see both of you later." With as much dignity as she could command, she walked out.

When she was safely in her car, Sheila gripped her hands together and sat very still to conquer her shaking. Estelle was furious, and her voice must have carried to the neighboring tables. Still, if she saw Mike again, word would spread anyway. She wasn't ashamed of being seen with him, but she wished Estelle's views hadn't been so public.

Turning the key, Sheila heard the motor purr responsively. As she drove home she thought about this new turn her life had taken. She had never realized such a rigid class system could exist in this day and time, though she had unwittingly been a part of it all her life. Mike was intelligent, gentle, loving—all the things a woman wanted in a man. How could anything so superficial as his family name and occupation bar her from dating him? It couldn't, and it wouldn't, she decided as she drove through the streets of Falls River.

Estelle didn't go straight home. She was much too upset for that. Instead she dropped Gail off at her house and drove back to Ed's office.

Ed Simon was the senior partner in the law firm of Simon, Schuler and Bates. At first glance Ed was an unimpressive man of average height and build and possessed a receding hairline. On second look, his piercing gray eyes and stubborn chin became noticeable. Ed seldom lost a case in court, and not many people could best him in a direct challenge. Estelle was one of the few.

She breezed past Ed's secretary and into his oak-paneled office. Ed looked up from the stack of papers on his desk as Estelle tossed her purse into one chair and sat in the other. "You'll never guess what Sheila is up to now," Estelle said without greeting him.

"She's refusing to appoint you head of the Research Foundation?"

Estelle waved her hand in dismissal. "She's still thinking about that. No, this is something worse."

Ed laid down his silver pen and leaned back in his leather desk chair. He knew there was no point in asking what had happened or in requesting that Estelle be brief. Estelle always took her own time as if no one else's day was as important as her own.

"She's seeing a Barlow!"

"Oh?" Ed asked in his best professional voice.

"His name is Mike Barlow and he runs an automobile repair shop, of all things!"

"Barlow," Ed mused noncommittally.

"He's the same one who pulled her out of the snow during the storm." Estelle got up and paced over the lush brown carpet. "Word must be all over town by now! We'll be the laughingstock of Falls River!"

"I hardly see how—"

"You never see anything!" Estelle snapped. "Didn't you hear me say who and what he is? How could Sheila do such a thing after being married to George?"

Ed refrained from comment. Instead he methodically filled his pipe while Estelle enumerated George's sterling traits.

"And now she's seeing this...this man!" Estelle leaned forward over the desk. "Something has to be done about it."

"What? Sheila is a grown woman."

"You're a lawyer. Think of something!"

Ed lit his pipe.

"There must be some way of preventing Sheila from dragging our name down like this!"

Ed knew better than to remind his wife that his name, and hers, too, was Simon, not Danforth. "She can see anyone she pleases. It's a free country."

"I hate it when you spout platitudes."

"Nevertheless, it's true. If she were defiling your name personally it would be different, but she isn't. You have no case."

"Maybe not legally," Estelle persisted, "but I do morally. She can't do this! What if she actually *marries* this person?"

"She's talking marriage?" Ed asked in surprise.

"Not yet, but what if she does? A Barlow would go to any lengths to get the Danforth money. Even to marrying Sheila!"

Ed personally didn't think marriage to Sheila would be such a great sacrifice, but he was too smart to say so. He puffed on his pipe; the aroma of his specially blended tobacco filled the room.

"If we can't stop Sheila, we have to stop Barlow!"

"Estelle, I have all these briefs to review before tomorrow," Ed said with practiced patience.

"This won't take long. We have to get rid of Barlow."

"Wipe him out?" Ed asked mildly.

"Don't be ridiculous. We'll buy him out. Those Barlows are a money-grubbing lot. Go to his garage and buy it. Today."

"Estelle," he began.

"Quit arguing with me. You don't have a better idea."

With a sigh, Ed laid down his pipe. If he didn't do as she said, Estelle would be here all day, and he didn't have the time to waste. "All right. I'll take care of it."

Mike whistled as he adjusted the carburetor of the Chevy Citation. Work was going well, and with any kind of luck he would be free to tinker with his ancient Ford coupe by midafternoon. Already his mind was on the source of the engine's persistent ticking. Not for the first time, Mike wished he had the leisure to work on his old cars anytime he pleased, or that he had the money to set himself up in the business of restoring them for a living. He had always been gifted at taking an ailing motor and making it run like new.

He finished his work on the Chevy and straightened as he critically studied the engine. He might prefer the antiques, but off-the-street repairs put the bread on his table. He slammed the hood, and the noise echoed against the concrete walls.

"Mike?" Carl called out, leaning through the office door. "Somebody here to see you. Mind if I go get some lunch?"

"Sure, Carl. And while you're out, will you run over to Mapleton and pick up that order I called in to Swain's? It's a gasket set and a couple of belts."

"Sure thing, Mike."

Was it Sheila who had come to see him? For a minute hope sparked in his golden-brown eyes. No, she wouldn't be back so soon. He suspected she meant it when she said he would have to call her. He wiped his hands on the rag that dangled from his back pocket and went to the office.

A well-dressed man stood gazing out the window. Mike suppressed the twinge of disappointment he felt and stuffed the grimy rag back in his pocket. "You're looking for me?" he asked pleasantly.

Ed Simon turned and gauged Mike Barlow before he spoke. He was younger than Ed had expected and had a more open expression. Ed had always prided himself on being able to read a person's expression and figure out his ulterior motives, but this man's face was as open as if he had no sinister designs at all. In fact, he appeared amiable and was nice-looking in a rugged sort of way.

Ed Simon assumed a no-nonsense courtroom demeanor. "I'm Edward Simon of the Simon, Schuler and Bates law firm."

Mike nodded his recognition of the firm and waited to see what the man wanted.

"We've never met, but I thought it was time we did." Ed smiled frostily as he looked directly into Mike's eyes, trying to get Mike to drop his gaze first.

"I believe you know my sister-in-law, Sheila Danforth."

"That's right." Mike met the lawyer's gaze unflinchingly as he wondered what this was all about.

"We, the family that is, were wondering if you two are seeing each other often."

"Why do you want to know?" Mike leaned on the edge of his battered desk and crossed his arms over his chest.

"Sheila, as you are probably aware, was widowed fairly recently, and she is still at a very vulnerable time in her life."

"Oh?"

"Naturally, I'm not suggesting that you would take advantage of her." Again Ed gave Mike his frigid smile.

Mike waited silently, not giving the other man the slightest advantage.

"We feel, my wife and I, that a woman in Sheila's position might make a . . . hasty . . . decision. One she might regret later."

"Sheila struck me as a woman who's quite capable of handling her own affairs." Mike's voice was cold and steady.

Ed had trouble hiding his surprise at Mike's educated choice of words. Obviously Mike didn't talk or act the way Ed had expected him to.

"Still, you can appreciate our concern," Ed emphasized. "We care for Sheila and want what's right for her."

"By whose definition?"

"I beg your pardon?"

"I care for her, too. Are you suggesting I would do something against her best interest?"

"No, no," Ed said quickly. "I only wanted to let you know that she has a family behind her all the way."

"Exactly why are you here, Mr. Simon?" Mike's words were clipped, the deeper tone of his voice signaling a warning.

"Actually I came on a different errand. I want to buy your garage."

"Why?"

"Come now, name your price. We're both businessmen."

"It's not for sale."

"Everything is for sale," Ed stated flatly. "It's just a matter of setting the right price."

"I'm not. And that's what you're really trying to buy."

"I don't know what you mean."

As Mike uncoiled and strode forward, Ed unconsciously backed up a step. "Cut the bull, Simon. We both know what you're saying. You're trying to bribe me not to see Sheila again."

"Bribe is an ugly word," Ed protested.

"So are several other names I could put to it. You can forget it, though, because the garage isn't for sale. Especially not to a Danforth. I'd burn it to the ground first. As for whether Sheila and I see each other," he continued menacingly, "we'll see each other for as long and as often as we please." He kept moving toward Ed as Ed backed into the door. As Mike towered over Ed Simon, he said, "Got it?"

Ed straightened, and the steely glint returned to his eyes. "Be careful, Barlow. Don't push me too far on this."

Although Mike smiled, he looked even more dangerous than before. "I never put a hand on you. You offered to buy my garage, and I turned you down. That's all that happened here, isn't it?"

Ed nodded slowly. This was not a man to be dealt with lightly. Instead he reached behind his back to open the door. "If you change your mind, the offer still stands. I'm willing to pay generously."

"I'll bet you are. So long, Mr. Simon. It's been interesting talking to you." Mike jerked the door open and glared at Ed until the man hurried away.

Slamming the door, Mike strode back to the desk. He still couldn't quite believe what had just happened. This dried-up little lawyer thought he could bribe Mike into not seeing Sheila again. "Damned Danforths," he muttered darkly. Everyone in the damned family was just as prejudiced and hypocritical as he'd predicted they would be—except for Sheila. She was like a rose in a patch of nettles.

He fished her number out of his pocket and yanked up the phone. Even if he didn't already care for her, he wouldn't stop seeing her now.

Sheila answered the phone on the second ring. She had been trying to read a novel but hadn't been able to keep her mind on it.

"You answer your own phone?" she heard Mike's voice say teasingly. "I expected one of the staff."

The mellow resonance of his voice brought a smile to her lips, but she detected a tightness underlying his tease. "I let Marie leave early today. She has a sick child." Nervously toying with a figurine she picked up from the table next to the phone, she said, "I was wondering if you'd call."

"If I hadn't, would you have called me?"

"I guess we'll never know now, will we? Are you all right? You sound odd."

"I met your brother-in-law today."

"Ed? Where would you meet him?"

"It seems he's in the market for a garage. He offered to buy mine."

The smile disappeared from her face. "He what?"

"That's right. You never told me that your family is in the car repair business. We have something in common after all."

"Don't kid about this. What happened?"

"Nothing. He made an offer. I turned it down."

Sheila was silent for a minute. Then she said, "I'm sorry, Mike. I had no idea he would do something like that."

"He also made it clear that he wanted me to stay away from you."

"Does this mean that you won't be seeing me again?"

"Look, nobody tells me what to do. I'm calling to ask you out."

Again Sheila paused. A tight knot was forming in her middle. "Why?" If he was seeing her only to show Ed he could, she would be crushed.

"I know what you're thinking, and it's not true. I want to see you. I was going to call you tonight." His voice sounded as though he was struggling with some emotion, but his words rang with sincerity.

"Are you sure?"

"Well, of course I'm sure. Why else would I be calling?"

"To show Ed that you can?" she suggested. When she heard Mike's suggestion of where Ed could go, she smiled.

"Are you going out with me, or not?" he demanded.

"How could I turn you down when you ask me so nicely?" She was laughing now. "Where are we going?"

"I thought we'd get a bite to eat and I'd take you to a car show. I don't guess you'd care about doing something like that."

"What's a car show?"

"Antique and classic cars. The vintage automobile club in Mapleton is having an exhibition this week."

"I'd love to go. When?"

"I close up at five. How about tonight at seven? Does that give you enough time? I guess your days are pretty well filled."

Sheila set the figurine back on the table. "I think I can squeeze you in between bridge clubs."

His soft laughter drifted over the line. "I'll see you at seven."

Sheila said goodbye and hung up. For a minute she sat staring at the phone. Ed had actually tried to chase Mike away. And failed. Since she considered Ed to be very formidable when he chose to be, her estimation of Mike climbed even higher.

By the time he rang the doorbell, Sheila had washed and dried her hair and was dressed in a pair of camel slacks and a pale gold sweater. She opened the door and greeted him with a smile.

His eyes lit up when he saw her.

She looked up at him eagerly. "Am I dressed right? I don't know what to wear to a car show."

"You look great." He took her parka from the chair beside the door and held it for her. When she slipped it on, his hands lingered on her shoulders as if he wanted to pull her into his arms.

Sheila felt her pulse quicken and hoped he would.

"I don't know what happens to me when I'm around you," he said gently, wrapping his arms about her and nuzzling the softness of her hair. "I think you have me bewitched."

"I was just thinking the same about you."

"Come on," he said, releasing her with regret. "I promised you antique cars and food."

When she saw his car, Sheila's eyes widened. "It's an old Mustang," she exclaimed.

"A '65. That's 'classic,' not 'old,'" he corrected her with a grin. "You were expecting my tow truck, maybe?"

"It's beautiful!" She walked around the car, admiring the apple-red finish and gleaming chrome. "It looks as if it just drove off the showroom floor."

Mike viewed the car with pride. "I've done quite a bit of work on it," he admitted.

Sheila let him open her door, and she sank into the bucket seat. The interior was black and even smelled as if it were new. They drove out of town and down the sloping hill toward the river.

When they crested the hill beyond, Mike turned into a familiar parking lot. Sheila leaned forward to read the neon light that spelled out Quick Stop.

He gazed at her to get her reaction. "Mind eating here? It's not Maxim's, but the food is good."

"I hear they make wonderful hamburgers," she said with a straight face. "And I know the grill is clean because I scrubbed it myself."

"Sheila," he said slowly, "I don't know how this is going to ever work out."

Their eyes met, and she read as much concern in his as she knew must be mirrored in her own. "Don't look so worried," she said, lightly. "Most schools of thought agree that sharing a hamburger isn't permanently binding."

They went inside, and Mike waved to a big man he called Sam, who was working behind the counter. He led Sheila to the booth where they had spent the night in the storm.

"This feels familiar," she said as she slid across the vinyl seat. "I think I've been here before."

The waitress, clad in a blue-and-white-checked uniform, came over to the table and handed them two dog-eared menus. "Hi, Mike. What're you up to these days?" she asked in a very familiar manner before her eyes sized up Sheila.

"Not much. Sam working you too hard?"

"That'll be the day."

Mike smiled at Sheila. "Hamburger?" She nodded, and he gave their order to the waitress.

"A friend of yours?" Sheila said as the woman left.

"Her husband is one of my regular customers." He studied Sheila's face as if it might hold a solution to the problem that was growing around them. Had he compared her to a rose? She was much more rare than that. He couldn't possibly hope to win someone like Sheila for his own.

"Is something wrong? Why are you looking at me like that?"

"I was just thinking that you may very well be the most beautiful woman I've ever seen."

A blush made Sheila drop her gaze. "I'm not accustomed to compliments. Thank you."

"It's true. And you'll have to get used to hearing me tell you so. Any woman as lovely as you are should hear it, and often." He covered her hand with his own.

Before Sheila could think of an answer, the big man from behind the counter came toward them. "Hey, Mike," he boomed, "broken into any cafes lately?"

"Hello, Sam. No. Not lately. I hope Jim Weller got your door fixed up. I swapped him a little mechanic time for his carpenter time."

"Yeah. He did just fine. Better than it was before. Thanks."

"Sam, I want you to meet my accomplice in crime, Sheila Danforth. Sheila, this is Sam Threadgill."

"Mike has told me about you," she said as Sam's beefy hand engulfed her own.

"He's been keeping you a secret," Sam answered. "I don't think I've seen you around."

"I guess we just never met."

Mike was watching her with pride. She had a way about her that was pure class. Every man in the room had glanced at her admiringly at one time or another since they'd walked in. Mike felt a slight touch of possessiveness. She was smiling at one of Sam's stock jokes that Mike had heard a dozen times and that she must have heard before as well. Or maybe the same jokes weren't told on Hazelglen Street. Sam told the punch line, and Sheila laughed with true enjoyment.

The waitress arrived with their meal, and Sam slapped Mike on the shoulder. "I like this one. Bring her back." With a wink at Sheila, Sam went back to work.

"What did he mean, 'this one'?" Sheila asked. "Do you bring a steady stream of women out here?"

"How's your hamburger?"

"Does that mean you do?" she asked. She was surprised at her jealousy.

"Not anymore."

He didn't elaborate, and Sheila was afraid to ask. She felt as if she was treading on quicksand. Surely she couldn't care as much for him as she thought. It was much too soon!

"What were you like as a boy?" she asked after a few minutes. "Have you always lived here?"

"All my life. I was like any other boy, I guess. I fished in the river and played hooky from school when I could, and generally grew up. Once I tried going over the falls in a canoe. That was a mistake. Luckily I can swim."

"I'll bet you were a real hell-raiser," she commented. "I can just imagine you."

"What about you? Did you live in a town like Falls River?"

"No, it was much smaller. More like Mapleton."

"I'll bet you went to a private school and wore ribbons in your hair and starched dresses."

"You're wrong. I was a tomboy." She didn't admit he was right about the school. Her parents had seen to it that she met only boys like George Danforth. "I would have lived on a horse if I'd had a choice."

"Let's see now," he mused as he finished his hamburger. "Kentucky, horses. Could it be your father raised Thoroughbreds?"

"Bingo! What a remarkable deduction." She supposed he would have had to know about her background eventually.

"Any Derby winners?"

"Only one. And that was years ago," she said as if that canceled it out.

Mike smiled wryly. "You're as wealthy as the Danforths, aren't you?" he said.

"Not quite," she hedged. "Does it matter?"

"Not as much as it did. I think I'm getting used to it."

"Good."

"The question is, can you get used to me being a working man?" He jerked his chin to indicate the worn linoleum, the vinyl booths, the cheap prints on the wall. "This is who I am."

"I think you're having a lot more trouble with that than I am," she said. "Who are you trying to convince?"

He studied her face before he swung out of the booth. She had such a knack of making all his objections seem insignificant. He gave the check and money to the waitress at the cash register as Sheila put on her coat. Surreptitiously the male eyes in the room followed her every move. She looked as comfortable here as if she ate at cheap diners every night of the week. Mike frowned slightly, wishing that she were as ordinary a woman as she seemed to be. It would make things so much simpler. But when he put his arm around her, he felt the luxurious fur, and the perfume that wafted to his nose wasn't the kind a discount store would carry. Mike had to face the uncomfortable realization that he really *might* be a snob, just as she had once said.

Chapter Seven

The vintage cars were on exhibit in a large hangar-like building just inside the city limits of Mapleton. Music from the big band era of the thirties and forties floated from speakers near the lofty roof, and spotlights sparkled off polished chrome and glossy fenders. Each car was parked on its own island of artificial grass and was cordoned off with velvet ropes supported from gleaming brass stanchions. Sheila had never seen so many antique cars in one place, and she was spellbound.

"Where do they all come from?" she asked in amazement. "I never expected to see so many."

"They're from all over. Vintage car buffs stay in touch with each other and join clubs to keep up with the latest news." He nodded toward a dun-colored Rolls-Royce with dark leather upholstery. "When these were made, each one was an individual work of art. If you look under the hood, you'll see the name of the mechanic who was responsible for this particular vehicle."

He guided her to a sleek black Ford with wire-spoked wheels. "The spare tires were often mounted on the running boards. See that cone-shaped thing hanging just inside? It's a flower vase. Just one of the options a buyer could add. The windshield can be tilted to change the airflow, but there are no side windows."

"Why not?"

"People were accustomed to open buggies. They expected to be cold when they traveled from place to place. Besides, roll-up windows were still in the future. A permanently enclosed automobile would be much too hot in the summer."

"You know so much about them," Sheila marveled as she admired the curving lines of a bright red Duesenberg convertible sedan.

"Vintage automobiles have always fascinated me. Even when I was a boy. If I had my choice, I'd work on them exclusively."

"Why don't you?"

"Money. It's as simple as that. My garage earns me a living, but it doesn't leave me enough free time to get into the more specialized work. If I took more time with the old ones, I'd have to turn down my regular customers."

"But if you enjoy it . . ."

"I also would need different equipment. The motor in that Packard, for instance, doesn't have much in common with the engine in your Mercedes. Besides,

Mapleton is more involved in vintage cars than Falls River. I doubt I would have enough customers there to make ends meet."

"You could always move here."

"Are you trying to get rid of me?" he teased.

"Not at all, but if you'd be happier doing something else, then I think you should do it."

"That's easy for a Danforth to say."

Sheila was quiet as she tried to decide whether he was right. She had always had the flexibility that money afforded. Not once could she recall doing without something for monetary reasons. "Maybe you're right," she conceded at last.

"I hadn't expected you to agree," Mike said, choosing his words carefully. "In fact, I was thinking that sounded pretty surly of me."

"You're right about that, too," she answered with a smile. When he frowned, Sheila laughed and took his hand.

As they wound their way through the cars, Sheila said, "Imagine what stories these old relics could tell."

"I can almost see Gatsby and Daisy going for a spin in that Bugatti Royale," Mike agreed.

"Gatsby and Daisy? You constantly surprise me."

"Garage mechanics are allowed to read Fitzgerald," he defended himself gruffly.

"Yes, but how many of them do?"

"I've always liked reading. After I graduated from high school, I had to help support my parents, and there wasn't enough money left over for college. Then, after they died, I felt too old to go back to school."

"You aren't too old."

He shrugged. "I'd feel silly. Anyway, what would be the point in it? I like working with cars, and I don't want any other job. When it comes to engines I'm already an expert." He put his arm companionably around her shoulders. "But when it comes to reading, that's a different matter. I'd rather read than watch TV, although I wouldn't admit that to just anybody."

"I like to read, too. See? We do have something in common."

He smiled down at her and hugged her lightly. "I think we have a lot more in common than that."

Sheila smiled and wondered if he meant to sound as intimate as he had. She was caring more and more for him and wished she knew exactly how he felt about her. She sensed a commitment from him, but he seemed as reluctant to put his feelings into words as she did.

As he gazed raptly at an Auburn, pointing out the distinctive vents on either side of its hood, Sheila tried to figure him out. Was the age difference a problem? Five years was quite a discrepancy when the man was the younger partner. Maybe that was one reason Mike was hesitant about his relationship with her. She didn't know who his other women friends might have been, but she was willing to bet they were under twenty-five. Age had never been something she worried about, but now she did. It was the one thing she couldn't change.

When they left the exhibit, a light snow was falling. The whispery sound of icy flakes touching earth and trees made the night seem even colder. They hurried to Mike's car and shivered as the heater hummed into life.

"Do you think winter will ever be over?" Sheila complained as she snuggled down into the warmth of her parka.

"It doesn't seem like it will be this year, does it? This has been the hardest winter in years."

As they drove back to Falls River, Sheila was unusually quiet. Mike kept up a one-sided conversation and wondered what she could be thinking about. She seemed to like the exhibit, but this was probably pretty dull in comparison to the dates she must usually have. Money had never been much of a problem for Mike. He had never had much of it, but he had never needed much, either. Sheila, on the other hand, was accustomed to it. How could Mike ever hope to keep a woman happy who was used to such wealth?

Keep her happy? Mike had tried to avoid it, but now the idea was blooming full-fledged in his mind. He wanted Sheila, and he wanted her on a permanent basis. He couldn't afford her, it was as simple as that. She couldn't be expected to live on his salary, and he wouldn't even consider living on her money. He quit trying to carry on a conversation and frowned into the night.

As they drove into town, Sheila broke the silence. "Don't take me home yet. Do you mind?"

"Of course not, but why?"

"I don't like that house. I guess that sounds silly, but it's like a museum. No matter how much noise I make, it's still so quiet." She looked over at him and watched as the succession of streetlights intermittently illuminated his face. "Where do you live?"

"I'll show you." He headed with determination toward his neighborhood. Surely this would convince her that their worlds could never meet. No one could ever compare his house with a museum.

The homes became less stately and more closely spaced as he turned down the streets that led him home. The trees were almost as old as the ones on Sheila's street, but there were many varieties, all planted according to the whims of each homeowner. They seemed rather haphazard when compared to the uniformly lined street that Sheila lived on. The styles of the houses were less varied the farther they went. In fact, all the homes in Mike's neighborhood had been built by the same developer and all had more or less the same design. Each sat with placid uniformity on a small patch of lawn. In the dark there was little to distinguish one from another.

"This is it," he said as he pulled into his drive. He turned to see if she looked appalled.

"How nice," she surprised him by exclaiming. "It's what they call a cottage style, isn't it?"

"I don't know. It's what they call inexpensive."

"Can we go in?"

Mike turned off the car and came around to open her door. "It's pretty small," he said defensively.

"I like it."

He tried to see it from her viewpoint. In the street-light's glow it was a study in pewter and silver. The roof sloped down over the entry, and the front porch was flanked by a row of bushes laced with the new snow. A curved sidewalk led from the drive to the front steps and was lined with another low hedge. It looked decidedly ordinary to Mike, and he wondered if she was just being polite.

He opened the door for her and took her coat as he flipped on the light. His furniture looked older than he had noticed before, and the coffee table could have used a dusting.

Sheila was looking at the bookshelves he had built on either side of the fireplace. "So many books! Why, you have your own library."

"I told you I like to read," he said defensively.

She went to the shelves as he knelt to start a fire. "We read the same books." She touched the spine of some favorites of hers and commented, "You can tell a lot about a person by the books he chooses."

Mike sat back on his heels as the fire caught and licked at the logs on the grate. "Come off of it. The house is small, the books are used to the point of looking seedy. I'll bet you've never been in a house like this in your life."

Sheila looked as hurt as if he had struck her. "The house is small," she admitted, "but if a book is well loved, it starts to look used. As for my being in a house like this before, you're wrong. My grandmother lived in one very similar to this, except hers was in the country." She knelt beside Mike before continuing. "My father *made* his money. He didn't inherit it. When my parents first married, they lived in a place much like this one. Mother was always ashamed of it, but my father showed it to me one day. He had a talent for making investments, and by the time I was born he was a wealthy man. I wish you'd stop holding that against me."

"I don't hold it against you," he denied quickly.

Sheila took a deep breath. "Is it my age?"

"What?"

"Is that why you keep pulling away from me for no apparent reason? Go ahead and tell me. I can take it."

Mike laughed in spite of himself. "You're worried about your age? How old are you?"

She lifted her chin defensively. "I'm thirty. Five years older than you are."

"So what?"

"Don't laugh, this is serious."

"No, it's not." He leaned forward and put his arm around her shoulders so that their foreheads touched. "I couldn't care less how old you are."

"Then what's your problem?"

"Your money. You were right the first time."

"That's all? That's why you act so distant at times?"

"Of course."

"That's silly."

"Not to me."

Sheila sighed. "Money isn't as serious a problem as my age."

"Your age is no problem at all."

"You're a very difficult person to understand," she confided, nose-to-nose with him.

"So are you. You worry about all the wrong things."

"I'm still cold," she reminded him in a serious tone, though her eyes sparkled. "Do you have any coffee?"

Mike stood and pulled her to her feet. "Right this way, my lady. I just happen to know how to make the best coffee you ever tasted."

Sheila followed him to the kitchen and watched as he went through the motions of making a pot of coffee. The house made her nostalgic for the cozy warmth of her grandmother's kitchen, but seen from Mike's perspective, it was small compared with her own home. The rooms were bare of the knickknacks and decorative touches of a feminine hand. Instead the house had a masculine, scrubbed-down-and-polished-off look—no frills or extras.

"You'd never be happy in a house like this," Mike said as if he had been following her thoughts. "Within a week you'd have cabin fever. Why, we couldn't even fit all your things in here."

Sheila caught her breath at the unspoken invitation. "Most of the furniture in my house has no meaning for me. I could sell it. If I had reason to, that is."

"I've seen your room. My entire bedroom would fit into your closet. You couldn't keep all your clothes in here."

"I've been meaning to clean out that closet," she replied, watching him closely.

"Look at this kitchen. No stainless sink or fancy oven. Most of all, no maid."

Sheila caught his arm and waited until he looked her straight in the eye. "Mike, what are you telling me?"

He drew in a long breath and let it out slowly. "You know I'm not interested in just having an affair with you. Hell, I don't even like the way it sounds. But how could we ever live together?"

"You could move in with me."

He laughed shortly. "Sure I could." Mike's voice was laced with sarcasm.

"Well, why not?"

"In the first place, I'm not about to live off your money, and that's the only way I could afford to live on Hazelglen Street. Second, Estelle and that lawyer husband of hers would have such a fit you'd never hear the end of it. Third, I wouldn't make it with your crowd. Fourth, my tinkering with those two old cars of mine would have the neighbors and probably the zoning committee up in arms."

"How do you know you wouldn't fit in with my crowd? You and I get along pretty well, I think. They aren't much different from me."

"Aren't they? I wouldn't bet on it."

"You don't even know them!" she retorted in exasperation.

"I know their kind!"

"That's as snobbish a thing as I've ever heard! Will you just listen to yourself?"

"Look, lady, I love you, and I don't want to see you get hurt. We haven't got a future and that's that!"

"What?" she asked in a small voice. "You love me?"

"Of course I love you," he thundered. "What else are we talking about? Do you think I talk about living with every woman who agrees to go out with me?"

Sheila ignored his blustering and smiled. "I love you, too."

All the fight went out of Mike, and he drew her to him. Silently they held each other, neither knowing how to express all that was in their hearts. After a long time, Sheila said, "We can work this out, somehow. We'll find a way." Her words were muffled against his chest.

"I sure as hell don't know how." He nuzzled her sweet-smelling hair and breathed in the fragrant aroma that was Sheila.

"Let me move in here and see if it's not okay."

"No."

"Why not?" she demanded, looking up at him.

Mike stroked the firm skin along the line of her jaw and gazed deeply into her troubled eyes as he searched for words to explain. "George Danforth gave you a museum. I'm not going to give you a cracker box."

"You're being foolish."

"It's how I feel."

"Let's sell both our houses and get something in the middle."

"I can't afford it and I won't—"

"I know, I know. How about if I get a job?" she asked in inspiration.

"What could you do?"

"I don't know. Now don't look at me like that. Surely I can get a job doing something."

"No."

"Why not? Other women work."

"Not when they have millions of dollars. It's not right, somehow."

"Are you sure you really want to work this out?"

Mike poured them each a mug of coffee, and they walked slowly back to the living room. The fire made the room seem even cozier, and he turned off the overhead light after tossing some pillows on the floor by the hearth. Sheila sat cross-legged on the floor and gazed into the leaping flames.

"I want to work out this problem," Mike said as he joined her and gingerly sipped his hot coffee. "But we have to do it in such a way that it can't cause us larger problems down the road. You've never had a job, have you?'' Without a word, Sheila shook her head in agreement. ''I thought not. It gets tedious, to say the least. It's hard enough to keep going to work, day after day, when you need the money. You'd soon resent the grind.''

''We don't know that for sure,'' she countered. ''On the other hand, you also don't know that it would be so distasteful to live off my money. You could work on vintage cars when you felt like it, and when you didn't, you could do as you please.''

''I like to work. It gives me great satisfaction to do a good job.''

''I might like it, too.''

''How can you be so beautiful and so stubborn all at once?''

''I was about to ask you more or less the same thing.'' Her voice softened. ''You really love me?''

Mike put down his coffee cup and placed hers beside it. Laying her back against the pillows, he leaned over her, his face bronzed from the firelight. ''Lady, I love you more than I ever thought it was possible to love. I've tried to ignore it and to argue myself out of it, but it just won't go away. Do you really love me?''

''Yes,'' she said as she reached up to trace the line of his chiseled cheek. ''At first I tried to pretend I was only lonely, but I knew better. From the time I first saw you in the light of your truck, I've felt something for you that wouldn't be denied. I've never loved anyone half this much, and the better I get to know you, the more I love you.''

His dark gold eyes studied hers as if he questioned her words.

"Never before," she whispered. "Not anyone."

He lowered his lips to hers and tasted the warm coffee flavor that lingered there. She felt small and delicate beneath him, and a surge of protectiveness welled up in him. This was his woman. The one he was meant for. Why fate had dealt them such a problem, he didn't know, but he knew what had blossomed between them was right.

"Somehow," he murmured in the shell of her ear, "somehow we'll work it out. I'll never leave you. I'm not sure I could go if you sent me away. Not anymore."

"I could never send you away," she replied. "Part of me would go with you."

Mike ran his hands over her gold sweater and slid his fingers beneath it to touch the velvety warmth of her skin. Her breasts swelled beneath his palm, and her nipples peaked eagerly. Teasingly he ran the tip of his fingers just inside the sheer lace of her bra and smiled when she arched toward him. "Do you want to go to the bedroom?"

"No, I like the fire." She laced her fingers in the deep gold of his hair and felt the sensuous texture. "You have the thickest hair I've ever seen."

"Must be my extreme youth." When Sheila laughed, he added, "Were you really worried about the difference in our ages?"

"I still am." Her voice was dreamy because his fingers were still teasing her breast through the gossamer layer of her bra.

"I'll tell you what," he bargained softly. "Since you think I'm the one that's supposed to be upset about you being older, you let me be the one to worry about it."

"I guess I could do that." Her eyes were closed, and she felt his fingers awakening nerves she never knew were there.

"In twenty or thirty years it won't seem nearly as great a difference as it does now."

"You plan to be around me that long?" she asked, opening her eyes in surprise.

"I don't fall in or out of love very easily. In twenty-five years this is my first time."

"Really?" she whispered. "What about the girl in Germany?"

"If I had loved her, we would have been able to work it out. We didn't even try. You're my first love. Scout's honor."

"I get the feeling you were never a Boy Scout. Not if you can do what you're doing right now."

"Sure I was. I have my explorer's badge," he said, grinning.

Slowly, as if each inch of skin he uncovered was a revelation, Mike removed her clothes. When she lay in the mound of pillows with firelight dappling her skin, he undressed and lay beside her. Resting on one elbow, he stroked the curves of her body from shoulder to hip, his gaze following the path of his hand.

Sheila trembled from excitement, but she forced herself to be still as her lover traced the undulations and planes that made up her body. His fingers drifted up from her waist and over the mound of her breast. Gently he rolled the coral bud of her nipple between his thumb and forefinger and smiled when she caught her breath in pleasure.

"You have a body that was made for loving," he told her. "See how you respond to my touch? I like that."

Slowly he bent his head, and his lips claimed the treasure his fingers relinquished. Sheila murmured her delight and raised herself to meet him, offering him all of her charms.

Mike supported her and flicked his tongue over the tense bud until she moved restlessly and stroked the hard curve of his back in growing anticipation. Gathering the pillows beneath her, he lowered her back onto them and let his hand caress lower. She willingly opened herself to him and called his name softly as he sought out her most feminine recesses.

Sheila felt as if she might explode as he continued his caresses. She moved with him in sensuous invitation, and when he entered her, she sighed in ecstasy. As he moved deep within her, time lost all meaning and her senses whirled faster and faster. Suddenly she cried out as she arched her body against him and collapsed into his arms.

"Mike," she gasped, her breathing labored, her heart pounding. "You're so wonderful! I never knew it could be like this."

"I love you," he murmured as he began to move once more in the rhythm of love. "And you love me. That's what makes it so good between us. I've never known anything like this either."

Again their bodies quickened, and this time when Sheila spiraled up the peak of love, he rose with her. Together they burst into ecstasy and soared in the rainbow colors of love. Still united, they drifted together as the world slowly came to a standstill.

"I love you," she whispered as she ran her hand over the hard swell of his muscled chest. "I love you so much."

"I love you, lady. Come what may, we're in this together. Somehow we'll work it out."

Sheila smiled and cuddled against his lean body. "We'd better, because I'm not leaving you. Like it or not, you're stuck with a millionairess." When he opened one eye and looked at her, she added smugly, "If you can tease me about your 'extreme youth,' I can tease you about my money."

"I guess that's fair," he admitted. Grinning openly, he murmured, "I just never knew you debutantes were so much fun."

"And I never suspected you young pups were so exciting," she retorted, running tickling fingers over his ribs.

Mike burst out laughing, and her voice joined his. Long into the night they held each other and talked about everything and nothing, their silence punctuated by kisses and caresses.

Chapter Eight

The next morning Sheila awoke slowly. Her mind wanted to cling to the beautiful dream she had been having, but her body became alert in spite of herself. Stretching languidly, she felt Mike's long body beside hers, and she came fully awake.

When the fire had burned itself out in the hearth, they had come to Mike's bed. But in the dark she had seen little of the room. Now she looked about with curiosity. The walls were painted a pale cream, and the cotton curtains at the window were a rich shade of brown. The furniture was old but not quite antique, and the hardwood floor was covered by a bright rag rug.

Sheila rolled over to face Mike and found he was already awake. He was lying on his side watching her, his hair tousled boyishly from sleep.

"You're as beautiful when you're asleep as you are when you're awake," he told her gently.

"How long have you been up?" She blinked to finish clearing the cobwebs from her mind.

"I woke up several minutes ago, but I didn't get up. I decided I would rather look at you."

"You've been watching me sleep?" she asked in surprise.

"You fascinate me, no matter what you're doing."

"I love you. Last night really happened, didn't it? You really do love me?"

"With all my heart." Mike brushed a stray tendril of hair back from her face and leaned over to kiss her. "I don't have to work this morning. It's Carl's day to open up. Will you spend the morning with me?"

"I'd love to."

"Do you want to take your shower first, or would you rather stay in bed a little longer?"

Sheila smiled, "Is there room in your shower for both of us?"

"If we stand very close together," he said with a grin.

She followed him into the bathroom. It was small and utilitarian with black and white tiles on the floor and pale green tiles on the lower half of the wall. Mike bent over to light the gas wall heater while Sheila opened the cabinet to take out two oversize white towels.

"I like your kitchen better than mine, but I have to admit that I prefer my bathroom," she told him as he adjusted the water in the shower.

"You don't have a bathroom—you have a ballroom with plumbing."

"I'll bet if we started looking we could find a house with everything we wanted."

"It wouldn't do us much good unless it came with a pot of gold in the closet."

"You're being pigheaded again," she pointed out conversationally.

"I'm being logical."

"With you that's the same thing."

Mike grinned at her and held the white shower curtain to one side so she could step into the cubicle.

When he joined her, she stepped into his arms and said, "My, it is close in here, isn't it?"

Mike reached around her and got the soap out of the tray. Holding her to him, he soaped her slender back and buttocks. Her skin felt slick and sexy beneath his hands, and when he bent to kiss her, water soared over them both.

Sheila rubbed the soap between her palms to make bubbles and spread it over his wide chest. Her touch was lighter than his and not at all efficient as far as actually getting him clean. But he closed his eyes and enjoyed the sensations of her hands sliding over his skin.

A fine dew of water droplets spangled their hair and hung on their lashes as they gazed lovingly at one another. "You're one fine lady," Mike said softly. "I've never known anyone like you before in all my life."

"Well," she teased, "you haven't lived all that long, when you get right down to it."

"I can't believe you're still concerned about that."

"If we can joke about it, maybe I can get over it."

"Good, because your age is the last thing I'm worried about."

"You'll just have to get over your hang-up about my money, too," she informed him, "because I'm not going away."

"You'd better not. I want you right here." He drew her closer and thrilled at the sensation of her soap-slicked skin against his. "Damn, you feel good!"

"So do you."

By the time they finished bathing, the hot water was growing tepid. Mike turned off the water and pushed the shower curtain aside to reach for the towels.

"See? In a bathroom this size, everything is at your fingertips," he teased.

"I'm convinced. I'll move in today." Suddenly Sheila was afraid she had overstepped the boundaries. She blushed and looked away. "I didn't mean for it to sound like that."

Mike wrapped her in the soft towel and put his finger under her chin to lift her face. "I wish you could, love."

"I understand." But she really didn't. If he loved her and she loved him, what was his problem?

They toweled each other dry and took turns blow-drying the other's hair. When they were dressed, they put on their coats and walked through the frosty air to the car. Sheila slid in beside Mike. "You still haven't told me where we're going," she said.

"I know. It's a surprise."

He drove through the neighborhood, and at the first convenience store he pulled into the parking lot.

"This is the surprise? I've seen stores before."

"Stay here. I'll be right back."

When he returned, he carried a bag that smelled of fresh-baked cinnamon rolls and also contained two large Styrofoam cups of coffee. "I know the people who own this place," he explained, "and they always finish baking about this time of the day. Here." He took a cinnamon roll as big as a saucer from the bag. "Don't burn yourself. It's hot."

Sheila took an experimental bite. "This is wonderful!"

Mike looked as pleased as if he had baked it for her himself. "Wait until you see the rest of the surprise."

"There's more?"

By the time they reached the edge of town, the cinnamon rolls were gone and the coffee was warming their insides. Mike drove down the winding road as Sheila tried to guess where they were going. After several minutes, he pulled over to the side of the road and stopped.

"This is it? Where are we?"

"You've really never been here before?" he asked.

"Where? All I see are woods." Ahead of them, the narrow road curved out of sight. On either side of the road was forest, the bare trees etched against the clear sky. Pristine snow lay over the gently swelling ground, broken only by bushes and tree stumps too tall to be covered.

Mike opened his car door, and they got out. He protectively pulled the hood of her parka to cover her more warmly and took her hand. Full of curiosity, Sheila followed him into the woods and down the gentle slope.

"In the fall these trees are really spectacular. All gold and red. In a few months the wildflowers will be everywhere. Not many people come here during the winter, though."

"Imagine that," Sheila said as she ducked under the snow-laden bough of a fir and nearly tripped over a bush.

In the distance she heard a roaring sound that she first thought was some sort of engine. As they neared, it grew louder. Rounding an outcropping of rocks, Sheila and Mike stepped out into a clearing, and she stared in awe at a cascading waterfall.

Torrents of water gushed over the bed of rocks, and gallons upon gallons tumbled and plunged in a headlong race to the river. Sheets of sheer ice coated the blackened boulders that confined the falls, and impressive icicles hung from all the nearby bushes and low trees. Above the falls, the far-flung droplets caught the sun in an opalescent rainbow against the azure sky.

"It's breathtaking," Sheila exclaimed. "I never dreamed this was here!"

"Why did you think it's called Falls River?"

"I just assumed it was named for those little falls at the edge of town."

"I can't believe you've lived here this long and have never been here or even heard of it."

"George disliked the outdoors, and I never considered going exploring by myself."

Mike pointed downstream where the banks narrowed and the water formed into treacherous rapids before flowing into the calm main river. "If you follow the bank around that curve, there's a swimming hole. Of course it's probably frozen over now, but in the summer every kid in town swims there. The trees have been thinned on this side of the water to make room for the picnic tables and swings."

"Could we go on a picnic there this summer?"

"Of course." He smiled at her eagerness. "That's what I had in mind." He looked back at the impressive waterfall. "I just wanted you to see it in the winter as well."

"I'm glad you brought me here." She stepped closer to him and put her arm around him. "This is like a wonderland with the ice and snow. And that rainbow!"

"It's a little something extra," he admitted. "You can't always see it. We just happened along at the right time of day."

"Every time we come here, I'll see the rainbow whether anyone else does or not. You know, it's like a special promise to us that everything will work out."

Mike gazed down at her hopeful face and smiled. "I hope so."

They walked slowly back up the hill toward the car, their breath making a wreath of fog whenever they spoke. Sheila had never felt as close to anyone as she felt toward Mike. Not even Gail made her laugh as easily or feel so safe in confiding her dreams and hopes.

The thought of Gail made Sheila feel a twinge of guilt. All her thoughts these past few days had been for Mike, and she hadn't called her close friend. Gail had never actually voiced any objection to Sheila dating Mike, but her disapproval was evident.

Sheila tried hard to understand Gail's attitude, but it was difficult. She honestly believed that if Gail had fallen in love with a man—no matter who he was—that she would have given Gail her unwavering support. Gail seemed to view Sheila's love for Mike as a pleasant but casual fling that would soon burn itself out.

Was she right? Sheila put her arm around Mike's waist and matched her steps to his as they crunched across the virgin snow. This had all come about so quickly! Who ever would have guessed that she, Sheila Danforth, would ever fall in love at first sight? Or that it would be so all-consuming? Her grandmother had been fond of old sayings, and Sheila could almost hear the old woman: "The brighter the fire, the quicker it's out." Would this hold true for Mike and herself? She had no way of knowing.

"How do we know our love will last?" she asked him, pausing beneath a huge sycamore.

He put his forearm on the smooth white trunk and leaned toward her. "There are no guarantees. There never are with love."

"But it's all happening so fast!"

"Do you want me to back off? We can slow it down if you feel it's necessary."

"No, that's just it. I don't want to slow down at all. I want to run toward it and grab all I can with both hands and wrap your love all around me."

"That's how I feel, too."

"Are we fooling ourselves into believing this is real?"

"Do you have any doubts?"

"Not even the hint of one. That's what scares me. Maybe I'm not being objective enough."

"Logic and love seldom go hand-in-hand." He drew her to him and rested his cheek on the fur of her hood. "I've had these thoughts, too. And I've decided to go for it. I love you, and I'm absolutely positive that we belong together. Love is far too rare to waste. We aren't hurting anyone else by our loving, and I see no reason to pull back. If I'm wrong and it burns out, well, we will have had this much.''

"I love you," she whispered into the warmth of his chest. "And I feel the same way. Let's go for it."

Arm in arm, they walked back to the car. On the drive back to town, neither spoke much, but they held hands, and the silence was as companionable as any words they might have shared.

Falls River was awake and bustling as Mike drove Sheila home.

Estelle had slept late as she usually did, but she roused herself enough to answer the phone by her bed. All her friends knew this number was her private line and that she slept late. For anyone to call so early on a Saturday meant it must be important. Groggily she pushed herself up in bed and mumbled a hello.

"Estelle?" her friend Nita Rockwell's voice sang out. "I didn't wake you, did I?"

"No, no." Estelle stifled a yawn and pulled the covers over her white satin negligee. "What's going on?"

"Oh, the usual. I had to get out early today. You know the benefit for orphans of policemen is tonight, and as program chairman of the Forum I had to be sure that all is ready. And it's a good thing I did. The help hasn't even emptied the trash in the kitchen, and I specifically told them to do that yesterday."

Estelle closed her eyes and ran her fingers through her shaggy hair. Surely Nita hadn't called just to vent her complaints about the cleaning staff at the Forum Building. Not this early in the morning.

"While I was driving home I came down Hazel-glen, and you'll never guess who I saw!"

Estelle's eyes opened to slits. "Who?"

"Sheila! And who do you suppose she was with? That man who owns the Barlow garage!"

"Oh?" Estelle was wide awake now and squinting to read her bedside clock without the aid of her contact lenses. "I suppose Sheila has car trouble again," she suggested hopefully.

"At this hour?" Nita laughed. "Honestly, Estelle, you can't believe that. I had heard gossip that she was seeing him, but naturally I never believed it. Not Sheila Danforth and a garage mechanic! But there they were, obviously returning home from having spent the night together."

"Come now." Estelle forced herself to laugh as though such a thing were absurd. She could never admit that she suspected it too and hadn't done anything about it. "Sheila would never do such a thing. I tell you, she's had trouble with that Mercedes before. I keep telling her she should trade it in for a new one."

"Where on earth could Sheila be going at this time of the morning for her to have car trouble?"

"Well, *you* were out this early, Nita. She may have had just as good a reason as you did."

Nita paused for several seconds. "I suppose you're right." Her voice was a shade cooler.

"Trust me, Nita. Sheila is a Danforth. We don't date garage mechanics. Really! I can hardly believe you would even suggest such a thing."

"You're right, of course. It just struck me as odd at the time. Well, I'll let you get back to whatever you were doing. Bye."

After the woman had hung up, Estelle continued to hold the receiver as her blue eyes glinted dangerously. Then she slammed it back in its cradle and jumped out of bed. Muttering angrily, she yanked on the negligee's matching robe and thrust her feet into her satin slippers. Taking up the phone again, she savagely punched out Nita's number. The busy signal confirmed her worst fears. Nita hadn't believed her explanation for a minute and was even now spreading the word about Sheila and Mike Barlow.

"Ed!" Estelle called out as she rushed toward the door that separated their rooms. "Ed, wake up!"

Her husband was already up and dressed in the slacks and golf shirt he always wore at home, even when his beloved golf course was under snow. "Don't shout, Estelle," he said mildly. "I'm right here."

"That was Nita Rockwell on the phone." Estelle was fuming. "You'll never guess what she told me! She just saw Sheila and the Barlow man—coming home!"

Ed merely looked at her over the top of his morning paper.

"Didn't you hear me? Sheila is shacking up with that man!"

"Really, Estelle. Where do you get those words? Television?"

She grabbed the paper and threw it to one side. Ed's eyes grew cold as he struggled to contain his anger. "Put down that paper and pay attention!" she screamed, her face barely inches from his.

"Don't push me too far," he warned her. "One of these days you're going to throw one of these tantrums and find yourself alone."

"Will I? I doubt it," she sneered. "Not when so much of your practice depends on my friends."

Ed didn't change his expression from that of aloof boredom, but his eyes were pale and as unyielding as flint. Only his suspicion that what Estelle had said about his thriving law firm might be true kept him from divorcing her. That and habit. Ed Simon was a man of deeply ingrained habits, strengthened by single-mindedness. He hated change, which also served to keep him married to Estelle. Successful lawyers handled divorces; they didn't get divorces for themselves.

"One of these days," he said with deceptive calm, "you're going to forget and talk to me like this in public. If you ever do, I'm leaving."

Estelle pushed away from his chair and paced as she always did when she was furious. She had heard Ed's threats for years and didn't believe him. "I can't believe Sheila is flaunting this affair so openly! Nita actually *saw* them. Can you imagine? Sheila coming home at this time of day!"

"How does Nita know they didn't go somewhere earlier? Just being seen together in the morning doesn't mean they spent the night together."

"Don't be so stupid! Of course they spent the night together."

Ed laced his fingers over the slight swell of his middle and glared at his wife.

She didn't look at him as she continued pacing. "We have to go talk some sense into her."

"Sheila is a grown woman and free to do as she pleases."

"She isn't free to stain our reputation in this town! Right this minute Nita is spreading her vicious gossip to all our friends!"

Ed sighed. Estelle might call them friends, but to Ed they were, more importantly, his clients. That meant his business could be affected. "All right, we'll go talk to her."

"I'll go get dressed." Estelle ran from the room, her robe billowing behind her.

Ed stared regretfully at the paper that lay strewn about the room. The morning paper was a sacrosanct tradition with him. He didn't bother to gather it up; they had servants to do that.

As Sheila watched Mike drive away, she smiled lovingly and touched her fingertips to her lips. She could still feel the tingle of his last kiss. Dreamily she went inside and slipped off her coat.

Marie, her maid, glanced at her with scarcely concealed condemnation as Sheila hung her parka in the coat closet. Sheila realized Marie must have seen Mike kiss her and that she probably knew who he was. Keeping her voice level, Sheila said, "Good morning, Marie. How's your baby?"

"She's well, thank you. I sent her back to day-care." Disapproval was evident in the maid's voice.

"That's good. I expect company for dinner tonight. Could we have beef tournedos and perhaps a chiffon pie for dessert?"

"Yes, ma'am." Marie's lips were compressed to show her feelings. "How many should I cook for?"

"Only two. It will be Mr. Barlow and myself." Sheila waited to see if Marie would overstep her bounds, but the maid merely nodded and went about her work.

Sheila drew a sigh of relief. She knew she had a jewel in Marie and didn't want to lose her. But Marie didn't have the status of an old family retainer, and Sheila wasn't about to let her maid censure her friends.

She went upstairs and pulled off her gold sweater. She had felt conspicuous returning in the same clothes she had worn last night, even though Marie didn't know the difference. How did other women manage this? If she and Mike had gone out dancing or somewhere more formal, she would have looked very decadent returning in evening wear. Perhaps she could leave a change of clothes at his place for just such a contingency. Yet that made it seem so clandestine. Sheila finished undressing and put the clothes in the hamper before putting on fresh ones. All this could be so simple if Mike would agree to live with her.

The chime of her doorbell sounded from below, and Sheila stepped to her bedroom door to listen. When she heard Estelle's voice, Sheila's eyes rolled toward the ceiling. She really wasn't in the mood to discuss George's memorial fund at the moment. When she got downstairs, she was surprised to find Ed in the den as well as Estelle.

"Hello," she greeted them. "I didn't expect company this morning."

"Obviously. I hear you only just got home yourself," Estelle said bluntly.

The smile disappeared from Sheila's face. Ed looked uncomfortable.

"Well, is it true? Where were you?" Estelle demanded.

"I was with Mike," Sheila replied calmly, "although it's none of your business." She turned to close the door to the den and saw Marie moving hurriedly away down the hall.

"I can't believe you would do such a thing! And admit it!"

"Estelle, you seem to be under the impression that I need your permission to live my own life. Nothing could be farther from the truth." Sheila kept her voice calm, but only with effort.

"What Estelle means," Ed put in smoothly, "is that she's worried about you."

"Why is she worried about me?"

"The Barlows simply aren't our type. She's afraid he may be stringing you along for personal gain."

"He's obviously after your money, you fool," Estelle ground out. "Can't you see that?"

"Mike and I love each other," Sheila snapped back. "He isn't after my money!"

"I know you believe that," Ed put in, "but you can't really be certain."

"Yes, I can!"

"All we want you to do is be more prudent. Back off from this and look at it as dispassionately as possible. Don't you see how suspicious it looks? You didn't know this man at all a few weeks ago, and—"

"And now you're doing God knows what with him!" Estelle blurted out.

"Estelle, please!" Ed's courtroom voice commanded. "You'll only make matters worse."

Estelle glared at him as if she had something she would like to say to him as well, but held her tongue.

Ed continued. "Do you see our point, Sheila? We only have your best interest in mind."

Sheila looked from his patently concerned face to Estelle's angry one, then back again. "I understand what you're saying, but I still resent it. I know this has all happened very fast, but sometimes it does happen that way. I know you resent Mike because he's a Barlow, but I haven't always been a Danforth and I don't think that's a valid reason."

"That's not the only reason we resent him! He's a mechanic!" Estelle made the word sound like a perversion.

"He earns an honest living and is very good at his work!" Sheila retorted.

"Do you hear what you're saying? I wouldn't sleep with my gardener because he's good at planting tulips or a chauffeur because he's good at keeping a car on the road!"

"Neither would I!" Sheila's voice rose in volume to match Estelle's. She rarely lost her temper to the extent of shouting, but she wasn't about to back down. "I would love Mike if he was the bank president or on his way to congress!"

"Now, now. Let's not get so upset," Ed cajoled. "Estelle, sit down and be quiet."

Estelle glared at him and started pacing.

"Sheila, all we're saying is not to rush into something you may regret."

"He hasn't asked me to marry him, if that's what you mean!"

Estelle groaned and made a furious grimace.

"I should hope not," Ed said. "After all, you hardly know each other. Just don't do something that will require my service to undo." He gave her a fatherly smile.

"I hear you're going into the garage business yourself, Ed," Sheila said tersely. "Mike says you want to buy him out."

Ed's smile faltered. "He told you that?"

"Don't interfere in my life. Either of you. I've put up with a lot to keep peace because I hate conflict, but on this I stand firm. I love Mike, and if he'll have me I hope to marry him. If not, I want to live with him. Whatever I choose to do, it will be *my* decision. Do you both understand?"

"You've never talked to us like this before!" Ed gasped.

"See! I told you he was a bad influence on her!"

"Goodbye, Ed, Estelle. I've heard what you have to say, and now you know how I feel. I don't think we have anything else to say on the subject."

Sheila saw them to the door, and with a great effort she kept her face smoothly impassive. She detested conflict, but once she took a stand she was implacable.

Chapter Nine

By dinnertime Sheila was over her anger and concerned that she had revealed too much to Ed and Estelle. How much simpler it would have been merely to deny the entire matter. Just as it wasn't their place to meddle, it wasn't necessary for her to admit to anything. She should have simply shrugged their accusation off as idle rumor and averted the whole unpleasant scene.

As it was now, Ed and Estelle knew she had not only spent the night with Mike, but that she was hoping he would want to make their relationship permanent. This made her feel far too vulnerable for comfort. What if Mike never asked? Not only would she be without him, but they would know the depth of her rejection.

For dinner she dressed in a wool plaid skirt of heather blue and purple and a ruffled white cotton blouse. At her throat she fastened an antique broach of filigreed silver with a diamond in the center. On her ears she placed diamond stud earrings, then slipped on a sapphire ring.

When the doorbell rang, she hurried downstairs to intercept Marie. The maid had been sulking all afternoon, and Sheila didn't want Mike to realize the trouble she was having at home. Sheila could still scarcely believe the class lines that existed in Falls River. Obviously Marie respected the invisible boundaries as firmly as Estelle did. Sheila waited until Marie had headed back to the kitchen before opening the door.

Mike stood on Sheila's porch, smiling warmly. As she invited him in, Mike surprised her by pulling her impulsively into his embrace. As their lips met in a tender kiss that quickly swelled to passion, a flood of emotion swept all thoughts of propriety for Marie's sake from her mind. In Mike's arms, Sheila felt safe and secure. The musky scent of his after-shave filled her nostrils, bringing back a flood of tantalizing memories of the night before. As they mutually parted, their eyes held for a few moments before Sheila remembered that he still had his coat on and that Marie might come back in at any moment. As she helped Mike out of his coat and put it away in the closet, she noticed he didn't seem so ill at ease in the foyer's marble cavern as he had the last time he had been there.

Mike was taking all of her in as his eyes moved caressingly down to her feet then back up to her face. "You look marvelous tonight." He put his arm around her and walked with her toward the den. "Something smells good. I gather you aren't attempting spaghetti again?"

"No," she said brightly. "Marie is cooking tonight, so it's safe to eat." As soon as they entered the den, she wished she had chosen another room. She could still recall the morning's unpleasantness here all too clearly, and her expression reflected her thoughts.

"Is something wrong?"

"No," she denied quickly. "What could be wrong? Well, maybe one thing. Estelle and Ed know where I was last night."

"So?"

"They came over this morning, and, well, it got out of hand before they left."

Mike's lean jaw tightened. "I'm going to go have a talk with Ed Simon."

"No, no. Don't do that."

"He's upset you. I'm not going to put up with that."

"Ed didn't cause the scene—Estelle did. Take my word for it. It's better to let the matter drop."

Mike sat beside her on the couch and took her hand. "Sheila, there's something—"

"Let's just drop it," she said hastily. By the expression on his face she could see he was about to say something of grave importance. If he insisted that they not see each other again, she wasn't sure she could stand it. "There's the bell. Dinner is ready." She leaped to her feet and rushed him to the dining room.

The formal room was as impressive as a banquet hall and about as inviting. As Mike held her chair, Sheila wondered what she could do to make the house seem less stilted. No wonder he didn't feel at home here—it wasn't a home. It was a showroom for all the things George thought they should own.

Marie served the meal in silence that Sheila knew was stony but hoped Mike thought was respectful deference. As always the meal was superb, but Marie scarcely acknowledged Sheila's compliment.

When dessert was placed in front of them and Marie had left the room, Mike said in a low voice, "What's the problem with her?"

"No problem. She's just very shy." Sheila hoped her lie was convincing. If Marie didn't snap out of her huff, Sheila would have to confront her, and she had had all the conflict she wanted for a while.

"Sheila, I want—"

"How's your pie?" She was afraid Mike was going to suggest that they end their relationship in view of all the uproar their liaison was causing. "Marie's speciality is this lemon chiffon."

He tasted it and nodded. "Tastes great. There's something I want to say to you. I—"

"She also makes a wonderful blueberry tart," Sheila interrupted again.

"Sheila." He caught her hand and waited until she met his eyes. "Be quiet a minute. There's something very important I want to say to you. I've rehearsed it over and over all day, so hush and listen to me."

Slowly Sheila put down her fork. This sounded ominous indeed.

"I want you to marry me."

"Now, Mike, I won't sit here and . . . What?"

"I said I want to marry you. I've given it a lot of thought and even though it's sudden, I think it's the right thing for us to do. Why do you look so stunned?''

"Because I am!" Sheila exclaimed in a burst of joy. "I thought you were going to call it all off!''

"Why would I do that? I love you. Haven't you been listening to me the past few days?''

"Yes, but with all the trouble with Estelle and Ed and now with Marie . . .''

"Marie, too?"

" . . . I assumed you would want to back off.''

"You haven't answered me.'' His brown eyes searched her face with concern. "Does that mean you want to wait?''

"No. No, it means I want to marry you." She let him pull her to her feet, and she embraced him happily. "I love you so." Tears of happiness stung her eyes, and she laughed as she brushed them away.

Mike held her tightly. "Together we can handle anything that comes to us.''

"Even Estelle?"

"Especially Estelle. I still think I should have a talk with Ed.''

"When we break the news to them, I imagine we'll both have an opportunity to talk to him,'' she said wryly.

"He had better not give you any trouble. He has me to reckon with now.''

Sheila hugged him tightly and felt security and strength radiating from him. Never had she felt so protected and safe.

"We'll go look for a ring Monday. Carl can handle the garage alone. I want to find just the right one." He paused and added, "I can't get one to equal the one you had, but—"

Sheila reached up and put her fingertips to his lips to silence him. "I don't want an engagement ring. I would rather have just a simple gold band."

"I can afford diamonds," Mike protested. "I may not be a Danforth, but I can buy you a ring."

"You aren't listening to me. I don't want one. I had diamonds before, and they came to symbolize a loveless marriage. This time I want something entirely different. I want the steady, solid, dependable kind of love that I think of as a plain wedding ring."

"That's really what you want?"

"It truly is."

"Then it's yours."

"Now for the big decision. Where will we live?"

"We'll live here." His face and tone were determined but not pleased.

"I would rather live at your house."

"We've been through all that. I won't marry you and make you accept a lower life-style."

"With a little practice you could become pompous as well as snobbish," she observed.

"You're bullheaded enough for both of us," he pointed out.

"Okay, so it's still a draw on where we'll live. We can work that out later."

"Not much later. I don't plan on a long engagement."

"Oh? How long did you have in mind?"

"About a month?" he suggested.

"How about a week?" she countered.

"It may take us a month to figure out what our address will be."

"'Our address.' I like the sound of that. And I think Sheila Barlow has a much nicer sound than Sheila Danforth."

"So do I," he said with a proud grin.

When Marie came to clear away the dessert plates, they were still kissing. With a snort, the maid went back to her kitchen.

When Sheila said she wanted a simple wedding band, she had thought the choice would be easy. She didn't realize "plain" bands could be anything from smooth to brushed gold or silver and ranged in design from braided ropes of tricolor gold, through the gamut of Romanesque borders, antique Florentine, yellow and white gold mixed, to basket weave. They had exhausted the shops in Falls River that morning and had driven to Mapleton after lunch.

"All I wanted was a plain gold band," she whispered to Mike as the jewelry salesman bent to bring out yet another tray.

"You're going to wear it for the rest of your life, so we ought to look at all of them," Mike reasoned.

The salesman peered through his bifocals at the velvet tray and selected a ring. "This has been a very popular style."

"No chain design," Sheila said firmly. "I don't like the symbolism of being chained in a marriage."

"Perhaps this one?" He took out a tricolor ring woven into an intricate knot. "It reminds one of the tie that binds, does it not?"

"Yes. Too much so."

"What about this one?" Mike pointed to a wide one with a hammered-gold look.

Sheila tried it on and viewed it critically. "It's too wide."

"That's very popular now," the clerk replied.

"I can't bend my finger."

"We're running out of styles," the man said with scant patience. "Perhaps something in a diamond?"

"What about that tray in the corner?" Sheila asked, pointing through the glass.

With a barely concealed sigh, the man removed the tray he had out and replaced it with the one she had indicated. These rings were less expensive, and he was obviously reluctant to show them.

"There! What about that one?" Sheila exclaimed to Mike. The gold band was narrow with beveled facets along the edges that caught the light. Sheila slipped it on and gazed at Mike for his approval.

He smiled. "I like it."

"So do I. It's exactly what I'd hoped to find." To the salesman she said, "We also want to see the men's rings."

For Mike they selected a gold Florentine band with a beveled border that resembled but didn't exactly duplicate Sheila's.

"But they aren't perfect matches," the salesman objected.

"Neither are we, but it's what we want," Mike assured him. "Now for the inscription." He wrote some words down on a piece of paper, shielding it from Sheila's view. "Put this inside hers."

In like manner, Sheila jotted down a note and pushed it toward the man. "This goes on his. But don't tell him what it says. I want it to be a surprise."

The jeweler read first Mike's inscription, then hers, and looked from one to the other. "Neither of you knows what the other wrote?"

"No," Mike said. "We agreed to surprise each other."

"You will be," the man said dryly. "I can almost guarantee it."

They paid for the rings and were told to pick them up the following week. Hand in hand, they walked out onto Mapleton's main street. "I've always liked this town," Mike commented as they strolled back to his car. "Everybody seems so much friendlier here."

"Except that jeweler. He really wanted to sell us one of the more expensive rings."

"He probably commutes from Falls River."

Sheila smiled and drew a deep breath of air. "It's warmer today. Maybe spring will come after all."

"Let's drive around for a while before we go home," he suggested. "Unless you have something else to do today."

"I'd planned to be with you."

"I like the sound of that."

They drove through the residential sections of Mapleton and dreamed as lovers always have about what sort of house they might own someday. Mapleton was an old town, even older than Falls River, and many of the houses had the elegant lines of a gentler time. The most exclusive section had huge houses placed well back from the road and evidence of professional landscaping.

Flanking the most elite section was an older neighborhood. The houses here were mostly Victorian and, while much less prestigious than those of a few blocks over, were surrounded by expansive lawns. Sheila leaned forward and pointed to a corner house with lemon clapboard siding, forest-green shutters and white trim. It sat on a broad, deep lawn with huge trees in front and what might be a small orchard in the back. The house had a wraparound porch on the ground floor, and a sitting porch on the second floor was neatly sandwiched between two Queen Anne turrets. Both porches and the eaves were laced with white gingerbread trim, and the room between the turrets had a jewel-like round window. On the front lawn, beside the curving brick walk, was a For Sale sign.

"Stop the car!" Sheila exclaimed.

"What! Did I hit something?" Mike slammed on his brakes and looked around.

"That house! Just look at that house!"

"Damn, Sheila. You scared me half to death." He pulled over to the curb and looked across the street at the graceful house.

"Isn't it perfect?"

"It's a beauty all right."

"Let's look at it closer."

"We can't do that!"

"Why not? It's for sale."

"Someone may live in it."

"I don't think so. It has a lonely look."

"Someone shoveled the walk."

"Realtors sometimes have that done so prospective buyers can get to it." Sheila opened her door and got out. "Are you coming?"

Mike wasn't sure about all this, but he followed her across the street. He, too, was fascinated by the house. It looked like something out of a particularly pleasant daydream.

Sheila went onto the porch and rang the bell. When no one answered, she cupped her face between her hands to gaze past the lace curtains into the house. "It's empty," she reported. "I thought so."

They circled the house, trying to guess at the layout of the rooms and what might be upstairs. "It's a lovely house," she said with a sigh. "It's perfect just the way it is. What do you suppose the owners are asking for it?"

"I don't know, but I'll bet it's not cheap." Mike had rarely seen a house he liked as much as this one. It even *felt* good. He reminded himself to be practical.

"Let's look out back." Sheila led him across the yard and past the group of trees that did indeed appear to be fruit trees. A hedge circled the garage and back lot, but it was the garage that caught Mike's attention.

There were four bays for cars, and one of them opened to a workshop area. A wide expanse in front of the building was paved, and it was all virtually hidden from the street.

"I guess it was built for a family with a number of teenagers," Sheila surmised. "Who else would need room for so many cars?"

"I would," Mike replied with growing excitement. "There's plenty of space here to restore vintage automobiles and still have room for our own cars." He shook his head. "What am I saying? This house must be way out of my price range."

"It's not out of mine," Sheila suggested hopefully.

"You know how I feel about that."

"But you just said it's perfect!"

"It is, but I won't buy a house I can't afford." His voice was as unhappy as Sheila looked. "Come on, sweetheart. We'd better be going."

Reluctantly Sheila nodded. But as she passed the realtor's sign she memorized the number.

When Mike dropped her off at home, Sheila called the realtor in Mapleton and asked the price of the house. While it was very reasonable, it was more than she knew Mike would want to spend. Thanking the woman, she hung up.

Trying to put the house out of her mind, Sheila decided to go see Gail. So far she had told no one of her engagement, and she wanted her best friend to be the first to know.

Gail lived two blocks away in a rambling one-story that had lines similar to a Frank Lloyd Wright home. Sheila had always considered the house too austere for her own tastes, but Gail had pointed out that in Falls River the choices were rather limited.

Sheila was admitted by Gail's maid and was shown into the cavelike den. The room was large and had lines more like an adobe hacienda than a house in Connecticut. The walls that separated the den from the living room on one side and the study on the other were free-form plaster dividers that contained planters. An unlikely arrangement of stuffed saguaro cactus made of white canvas was grouped in one corner— a reminder that Gail's former husband had earned his fortune, and thus Gail's alimony, in Arizona.

Gail and another woman were seated on the leather couch. When Sheila entered the room, Gail smiled and motioned for her to join them.

"Hello, Julia. I didn't realize you had company, Gail, or I wouldn't have dropped in."

"Nonsense. You're always welcome. Coffee?"

"No, thanks."

Julia Overton leaned forward to flick the ash from her pastel-colored cigarette into the cut-glass ashtray. Her hair was an unlikely shade of black and fit her small head like a sleek cap. Her features were pinched and grouped toward the front of her face, giving her a sharp, feral look. "I haven't seen you in ages, Sheila. Where have you been?" She drew on her cigarette and pursed her scarlet lips to send a jet of smoke upward.

Sheila hesitated. Julia was one of the crowd that she liked the least. She had never understood Gail's friendship with her. "The snow has kept me pretty close to home."

"That's not all that has," Gail said teasingly.

"Oh?" Julia's black eyes darted to Sheila. "What does that mean?"

"She means I've been seeing someone. I doubt you know him."

"His name is Mike Barlow. I saw him downtown yesterday, and he's gorgeous."

"Barlow. I don't think I know that family. Are they from around here?" Julia asked.

"Yes. The Barlows have been here longer than the Danforths," Sheila said as she took a cup of coffee from the sideboard.

"She's been seeing a great deal of him," Gail put in. "I keep telling her we should all get a chance to meet him."

Sheila smiled and settled back onto the couch's plump cushions. "As it turns out, you will. You see, we're getting married."

The smiled faded from Gail's lips, and Julia leaned forward expectantly. "Married?" they chimed, almost in unison.

She couldn't understand why Gail was staring at her like that, and why she was suddenly so quiet.

"You're not wearing an engagement ring," Julia said after an awkward pause. "Perhaps it's not official?"

"It's official, all right. We bought the wedding bands today. I didn't want an engagement ring."

"You bought rings? Today?" Gail gasped.

"They're being engraved now."

"Wedding bands. I suppose there is a trend toward that sort of thing." Julia glanced at the massive knot of diamonds on her own left hand. "I've seen some bands of emeralds and diamonds that were quite attractive."

"I chose a plain band," Sheila corrected.

"When are you getting married?" Julia's eyes glittered as if she might be laughing on the inside.

"Next month. We haven't set the exact date yet."

"Well!" Gail gushed brightly, clenching her hands together. "We'll have to celebrate. I'll give you a shower."

"For a second wedding?" Julia scoffed. "I don't think that's done."

"A party then. I'll give you an engagement party."
Gail was talking a bit too fast and smiling a bit too
much.

"That would be lovely," Sheila said hesitantly. She
had felt an instant reservation about the idea but could
do nothing but accept the offer.

Julia leaned back on the opposite couch and crossed
her twiggy legs at the knee. "Tell me about this man.
Mike Barlow, was it? What sort of business is he in?"

"He has a garage."

"How can he make much money doing that?"

"Really, Julia, that's pretty personal," Gail objected.

"Well, for goodness' sake, Gail. We're all friends
here," Julia protested.

"I think I'll plan the party for next Friday," Gail
said. "Will that be a good time for you, Sheila?"

"Wonderful. I'd like for Mike to meet my friends."

Julia raised her eyebrows. "You mean I'm not the
only one who hasn't met him? And he lives here in
Falls River?"

"I'll explain it all to you later," Gail said in a rush.

"Goodness! Look at the time!" Julia exclaimed.
"I've got to run. Bye, Sheila. I'll see you next Friday.
Gail, thanks for the coffee. Call me later?"

"Yes, I'll be talking to you."

Sheila waited until Gail escorted Julia out and returned. "What is there to explain to Julia?" she asked
evenly.

"You know how Julia is," Gail evaded.

Carefully Sheila replaced the coffee cup on its
matching saucer. "I guess I'm a little disappointed in

your reaction to my news. Julia and I have never been close, but I expected more enthusiasm from you."

"Oh, for goodness' sake, Sheila. You just caught me by surprise. You can't drop news like that on someone and expect them to know how to react."

Sheila studied her friend thoughtfully. "I should think sudden news would be more apt to bring out how a person really feels."

Gail shrugged. "You know I'm happy for you. Now, about the party. Let's have it here. Say eight-ish? Formal?"

"Eight o'clock is fine, but I'd prefer casual dress. You know how stuffy formal parties can be."

"Okay. Let's say casual. I think I'll have Louise make up some of those pâté hors d'oeuvres that I served at the Christmas party. Champagne, of course, and a bar. Oh, and those petits fours from that new bakery we like so well. Louise can also make up some finger foods of some sort. What about music?"

"I'll leave the details of that up to you. Let's just keep it simple and not invite the whole crowd. Mike has never met any of our group, and I don't want him to feel overwhelmed."

"Of course not. We wouldn't want that." Gail pursed her lips thoughtfully. "Please don't take this the wrong way, but are you quite certain you know him well enough to marry him?"

Sheila leaned forward, her eyes shining. "I'm positive. Gail, I've never met anyone like him. He's interesting to talk to, fun to be with—everything about him is just right for me."

"Hmm. He sounds too good to be true."

"Maybe it's because I love him so much that his faults don't matter to me."

"But will they matter a year from now?"

"Like Mike said, there are no guarantees. I only know that when I'm with him I'm not only happy, but I like who I am. You know? He brings out a part of me that I never knew existed. I can be myself with him." Sheila paused. She was revealing a great deal to Gail. Up until now she had never realized that she wasn't always this open with Gail. Deciding she'd better cut this off before she said too much, she said, "We're good for each other and we're very sure this is the real thing."

Gail reached out and patted Sheila's hand. "Whatever you want for yourself, I want it for you, too."

Sheila wondered why she felt some reservation about believing her. Impatiently she shook off the thought. Of course her friends would like Mike. How could they help it? In no time he would be firmly established in her group.

Chapter Ten

I've been thinking," Mike said as they sat in Sheila's sun room, watching the birds outside hop about in the melting snow. "It wouldn't hurt to just look at the inside of that house."

Sheila looked up expectantly. There was no need to ask which house he meant. "That's true."

"Once we see the inside, we may not like it at all."

"I guess that's possible."

"The truth is, I can't get it out of my mind," he confessed. "I saw the way your face lit up when we were looking at it."

"So did yours," she countered. "It seems so perfect for us."

"On the outside at least. Let's just look at it. Maybe that will get it out of our systems. Do you remember which realtor had it listed?"

"Clermont, I believe," she said as casually as possible. They were going to look at the house! That meant Mike liked it as much as she did. Surely once he saw the inside he would agree to let her help finance it. She had no doubts at all that they would both love it.

Mike went into the den to call the realtor and soon reported that a Mrs. Allen would meet them at the house in half an hour.

The drive to Mapleton seemed to Sheila to take forever. The weak spring sun was trying valiantly to melt the snow, and sunlight glistened off the softening drifts. In her mind Sheila was already planning which of her furniture to keep and which to sell. She wasn't too surprised to discover she wanted to get rid of most of it. Above all, she wanted a fresh start.

"Now, sweetheart, don't get your hopes up," Mike said as he parked behind the realtor's car. "We're only looking."

"I remember." But her face was bright with expectancy. George had never consulted her about anything. Before his death, she had just accepted that way of life because she felt she had no recourse. But now, she and Mike were working together, and he valued her opinion. That was so important to her.

Mrs. Allen met them on the sidewalk in front of the house and held out her hand in a firm handshake. She was a tall woman with a large frame and a professional attitude. Her suit was black wool and looked expensive, and the blouse had tailored pleats that showed beneath her heavy black coat. The dark-rimmed glasses that sat on the bridge of her prominent nose were attached to a black velvet strap that draped behind her neck. Her hair was short, curled and a brassy shade of blond. Every inch of Mrs. Allen stated that she was a businesswoman. Sheila felt slightly intimidated.

"This is the Beall House," Mrs. Allen announced in no-nonsense tones as they climbed the front steps. "You'll find all the houses in this neighborhood are identified with names."

"Who were the Bealls?" Sheila asked as the woman inserted the key in the door.

"Couldn't say. Probably the first owners." She pushed the door open with the same flourish she might have used to uncover a rare jewel. Sheila and Mike followed her inside. "It's cold. Can't help that. Heat's shut off," Mrs. Allen explained in her staccato style.

Sheila looked about the broad entryway, and her smile deepened. On one side was a graceful stairway that curved up to the second floor. At the foot of the stairs was a bay window that would be perfect for plants. Opposite the stairs was a double doorway framed in white gingerbread. A hall led toward the back of the house.

She stepped into the front parlor and looked about as her spirits soared. The walls were papered with a reproduction of period wallpaper in silver, white and blue stripes. The woodwork was painted the same muted shade of blue. Lace curtains adorned the tall windows that went almost the full height of the twelve-foot wall. A fireplace with a beautifully carved mantel beneath a pale blue mirror sat in one corner. Sheila's eyes met Mike's, and they exchanged a smile.

"The mirror is wrong, I think," Mrs. Allen put in. "Blue mirrors were the rage in the thirties and this house is, of course, much older than that. I think 1886 is the date on my information card."

"I love the mirror," Sheila replied. "I think an old house should reflect the ages it's lived through."

"Naturally," Mrs. Allen responded, to be agreeable.

The floors were oak, darkened from generations of use, but Sheila could imagine them refinished and gleaming.

They walked through the dining room and back parlor that Mrs. Allen insisted on calling a den. The kitchen was huge and ran the entire width of the house. There was ample room for a breakfast table and all the cabinets anyone could need.

"Used to be a well here," Mrs. Allen said pointing at one corner. "Boarded over now." She peered critically at the sink below the wide window. "Sink's in good shape. Looks new. No refrigerator. You'd need to buy that. Stove stays." She nodded briskly at the large appliance.

A back stairway was in the hall just outside the kitchen, but Sheila insisted on going up the front stairs. On the large landing halfway up, there was a duplicate of the bay window she had seen below. The sunny area was a perfect spot for reading. A door at the top of the stairs led to the small upstairs porch. Across the porch was an identical door.

"Leads to the master bedroom," Mrs. Allen told them. "Right through here."

Mike led the way into the spacious room. The second story turret they had seen from outside made a round sitting area at the front of the bedroom. "How beautiful," Sheila exclaimed. The long windows were edged in stained glass squares through which the sunlight cast patches of color on the oak flooring.

Mike nodded, but didn't speak. He liked the inside of the house even better than he had the outside, but it was far more elegant than he had expected. He could picture its price rising with every room they entered.

A hallway connected the three other bedrooms. The two baths, according to Mrs. Allen, had been converted from yet another bedroom. Unlike the half-bath downstairs, these baths were spacious and tiled in a design reminiscent of the thirties. Mrs. Allen glanced around the master bath. "Good thing you like a house to show the eras it's endured. Looks like a flapper designed it."

Sheila smiled as she touched the pale lime and lilac tiles. "I like it." To Mike she said, "And it's big."

He looked at the oversize tub on claw feet and grinned. There was plenty of room for two in there.

They went down the back stairs, which were steeper and narrower than the front ones. Mike drew a deep breath and asked the question he had dreaded most: "How much?"

When Mrs. Allen gave him the asking price, he almost tripped. While it wasn't as expensive as he had feared, it was certainly more than he could afford.

Sheila gazed up at him expectantly. He looked away and said gruffly, "Let's see the garage."

It was all he had hoped it might be. The workshop was spacious, and the bays were open to one another, just as he would want them to be. "Will the owner come down on the price?"

Mrs. Allen shrugged. "It's a steal as it is. I'll ask."

"It's perfect," Sheila whispered to him.

"We'll think about it," he told the realtor.

"Don't wait too long. Won't be around for long at this price."

"We'll keep that in mind," Sheila said.

"Had another couple looking at it last week."

Sheila's fingers bit into Mike's arm and he had to work hard to refrain from flinching. "Let me know if the owners will come down on the price," he said, and wrote his name and number on the back of one of Mrs. Allen's cards. "Thanks for showing it to us."

Once they were in the car, Sheila said, "Someone else has been looking at it!"

"Realtors always say that."

"What if it's true?"

"Honey, you heard the asking price. I can't afford that."

"Together we could."

"You know how I feel about that."

Sheila sighed in disappointment. "I think you're the most stubborn person I've ever met."

He turned to her and cupped her face in his palms. "It's a matter of self-respect. People are going to say I married you for your money. I don't want our house to give them proof. Can't you understand that?"

"Yes," she admitted reluctantly. "But I don't agree. It seems like the perfect place for us to start a new life. A place that's halfway between Danforth and Barlow."

Mike drew her to his side and held her close. He knew she was right, but his pride wouldn't let him admit it. As perfect as the house was, he couldn't face knowing that Danforth money had bought it. The miles passed while neither seemed able to speak.

At her house, they parked in the driveway and sat for a few minutes. At last Mike broke the silence by changing the unspoken subject. "The engagement party is tonight. Should I pick you up at eight?"

"No, Gail wanted me to come over earlier. I'll take a cab. That way you can bring me home."

"Sheila, I'm sorry about—"

"Please don't talk about the house. Not yet. Give me time to get over this disappointment." She squeezed his hand to show him that she wasn't angry and was trying to understand.

A muscle tightened in Mike's jaw as he struggled not to give in. He hated to see Sheila disappointed in any way, but there was a lot at stake here. If she bought the house, wouldn't she also want to pay for furniture and carpets? Next she would want to buy their car and pay all the bills. Mike remained silent.

Sheila sighed and opened her car door. "Don't get out. I'll just see myself to the door. I have a dozen things I need to do before the party. Do you remember Gail's address?" When he nodded, she said, "Good. Don't forget that it's casual."

As she came around to Mike's side of the car, he rolled down his window. "I love you," he called to her.

Sheila smiled and leaned in to kiss him. "I love you, too. See you tonight."

By seven-thirty Sheila was in a cab and on her way to Gail's house. She looked at the bare ring finger on her left hand and smiled when she imagined the wedding band she and Mike had chosen. She could hardly wait to introduce him to all her friends.

At Gail's house she paid the driver and hugged her coat securely to her as she hurried up the walk. As usual, Gail had everything in perfect order, and also as usual, Gail was positive that she didn't. Sheila was accustomed to her friend's preparty jitters and almost automatically assured Gail that the flower arrangements were lovely and that the hors d'oeuvres would be delicious.

As Sheila looked at her friend hurrying about with her last-minute preparations, she thought that Gail's maroon velvet blazer over a pale pink blouse, with matching velvet slacks, were a bit dressy for a small informal gathering, but Gail was the hostess and the outfit was a new one that Gail had been longing to wear. When the first of the guests arrived and Sheila noticed how elegant Julia Overton's sequined sweater was, she looked back at Gail's chic attire and began to wonder if Gail hadn't told everyone that the evening was to be casual. But then she reminded herself that Julia frequently overdressed, and as her moment of doubt quickly subsided, she welcomed Julia with a smile.

By ten after eight a number of guests were there, but Mike still hadn't arrived. Sheila leaned close to Gail as the doorbell rang again. "How many did you invite?"

"You know how it is," Gail whispered back. "I couldn't invite the Armbrewsters without the Smyth-Talbots. And Julia asked if the Schulers were coming, and you know how close Catherine Schuler and Julia are. Then there were the Bates—I wouldn't dare have a party and not ask them. Gloria Bates would love to have a reason to rake my name through the mud.''

When the maid ushered in Nita and Harold Rockwell, Sheila raised her eyebrows at Gail.

"She's Estelle's best friend," Gail said in defense of herself.

"You invited Estelle and Ed?"

"Well, how could I avoid it? They're your family, and I had asked both his law partners."

Sheila managed not to groan, but it wasn't easy. The situation was already out of hand and bound to get worse before it was over. She plastered a smile on her face and hoped that Mike would show up soon.

Mike drove through the neighborhood in search of Gail's street. At the last minute, one of his best customers had shown up needing an oil change and lube job, and he hadn't been able to turn the man away. His watch showed eight-thirty, and he still hadn't found the house. He hated being late, but it was unavoidable. Besides, the streets in this section of town were so discretely marked that the names were almost impossible to read after dark. Being this late wasn't all his fault.

At last he found the street, a short one sandwiched between two cul-de-sacs, and he began the equally difficult job of hunting for the correct house. However, the large number of cars out front of one of them clued him in. Yes, it was Gail's house. He stopped in front, where he turned his keys over to a parking attendant. Trying to quell his apprehension, he headed for the door. He had never been to a party in a place like this, and he didn't know any of the people, except through his work. He had recognized several of the cars out front—the midnight-blue Lincoln had been in for a tune-up the week before, the Porsche was the one with a brake problem, the Cadillac had needed a valve job.

Nervously Mike tucked the back of his shirttail into his jeans and straightened his pullover sweater. There was no reason to feel so out of place. These were Sheila's friends. True, there were more cars than he had expected, but so what? He drew a deep breath and rang the doorbell.

When the maid opened the door, her eyes flickered over him judgmentally, but nevertheless she let him in. Mike gave her his heavy coat and stepped into the living room. Everywhere he looked, there were people. The men were dressed in sport coats and suits, and the women were wearing sequins and velvet. Thinking he must have somehow come to the wrong house, Mike turned to leave.

"Mike," he heard Sheila say as she caught his arm, "I was beginning to worry about you."

He turned to gaze down into her green eyes. Before he could reply, she said, "I want you to meet my best friend, Gail Taylor. Gail, this is Mike."

"Hello, Mike. I'm so glad to meet you at last."

He shook Gail's offered hand but found her handshake rather limp. "Sorry I'm late. I was held up at work and had some trouble finding the house."

"Held up? Surely you don't mean..."

"No, no. Nothing like that. One of my customers came in as I was closing and needed an oil change," he explained. He felt very uneasy that he had worn his jeans, but he was sure Sheila had said this was casual.

"Thank goodness," Gail gushed, pressing her hand to her chest. "For a minute I was sure you'd been robbed. How silly of me."

He didn't know how to respond; her inflection either implied that she thought crime was rampant on his side of town or that a garage wasn't worth robbing. Surely she hadn't meant to offend him, he thought. He was just a little nervous and defensive.

"Hasn't Gail decorated beautifully?" Sheila said, sensing Mike's tenseness.

Mike glanced around. "Nice flowers," he said with a grin. He had never felt so out of place in his life.

"Come with me," Sheila said. "I want you to meet everyone."

As soon as they were away from Gail, he muttered, "I thought you said it would be a small group."

"I thought it would be. I forgot that Gail never gives small parties."

"You also said it would be casual, didn't you?" He felt as if everyone in the room had taken note of his jeans and lack of tie.

"Gail said it would be," she answered. "Oh, here's Julia. Julia, I'd like for you to meet Mike Barlow. Mike, this is Julia Overton and her husband Frank."

Julia stepped closer to Mike than was necessary and took Mike's hand in a way that seemed more intimate than a handshake. The lights spangled off her ruby-sequined sweater but brought no glow to her pale skin. "Hello, Mike," she breathed in a contralto voice. She turned her sleek head toward Sheila. "Isn't this a divine party? Gail certainly has a way with people."

Mike extricated his hand as Frank boomed, "Don't think we've met. I'm Frank Overton." His handshake was a bone crusher, but Mike met it in kind.

"Glad to know you."

"Are you new in town?"

"No, I've lived here all my life." His grin was becoming forced, and he wanted nothing more than to leave. "I own Barlow's Garage over on Fourth Street."

Frank looked a bit confused. Sheila interrupted quickly. "Gail tells me you're about to remodel, Frank?"

Mike listened as the couple expounded on the impossibility of existing in their house as it was, and how perfectly marvelous it would be once they finished recreating it. Up until now Mike had never heard anyone speak of recreating a house. He guessed that these people must have little else to do other than make up hundred-dollar ways of saying common things. Mike tried to push aside his preconceived notions of how the rich really lived, but he couldn't. This couple seemed to fit the mold too closely.

Seeing the bored look in Mike's eyes, Sheila politely eased them away from the Overtons and into the thick of the crowd, where she began a seemingly endless stream of introductions. Faces and names blurred together in spite of Mike's effort to keep them all straight.

"Are these all friends of yours?" Mike asked Sheila when they were momentarily alone.

"Not really. I expected half this many and had hoped for less than that. Gail seems to have no self-discipline when she plans a party. She always ends up asking everyone she knows. But look at it this way—there won't be any others you have to meet later."

He grinned wryly. "I don't see how there could be." He wished he and Sheila could slip away. Although the party was in honor of their engagement, no one as yet had wished them well. Probably no one would notice they were gone. Only the knowledge that this affair was important to Sheila kept him from suggesting they go.

"I know they all seem overwhelming. I felt the same way when I first met them," Sheila told him. "After a while you'll put the right name to the right face."

He wasn't sure he wanted to know them that well, but he smiled and nodded. "I just wish I had known to wear a jacket and tie."

She shrugged. "I think you look great." A devilish gleam sparkled in her eyes. "You look better in tight jeans than anyone I've ever seen."

Her words made him feel much better, and he hugged her. She was so real, so down-to-earth. Surely he was misjudging her friends.

"Damn!" she muttered. "Estelle and Ed just came in."

"I see them," Mike said as his smile faded. Estelle's eyes met Mike's across the room, and although she quickly looked away, he had seen the pure venom in her glance.

"Maybe we can avoid them in the crowd. Let's work our way to the buffet table. I could use a glass of wine."

Mike personally thought a beer would be more palatable, but when they reached the table only champagne was to be had. Sheila handed him a glass and lifted hers in a salute. "To us," she said with a smile.

"To us." He drank the toast out of deference to Sheila but refrained from giving his opinion of the champagne. He could handle anything from beer to bootleg whisky, but champagne seemed like an affront to mankind—too fizzy to be taken seriously and too harsh to be enjoyed without acquiring the taste.

Sheila looked over the large assortment of hors d'oeuvres and picked up two triangle-shaped crackers smeared with a brownish substance that Mike thought might be pâté. She handed one to Mike.

Obligingly he tasted the cracker, forced the rest of it down and said it was interesting.

"Personally I thought it was just awful," Sheila confided in a low voice.

Mike laughed and winked at her. "So did I." When it was just the two of them, everything was fine, but Mike couldn't help but be aware of the subtle snubbing they were getting. He wasn't even sure that Sheila noticed, and he didn't want to spoil her evening by mentioning it.

Their conversation was interrupted by a loud voice from directly behind them. As Mike turned to see who was being so disruptive, he heard Ed Simon say to Frank Overton, "Yes, we were late getting here, Frank. I had to take the car over to Mapleton to be serviced. You know you can't get good work done here in Falls River."

Mike regarded the man coldly. Ed turned around toward Mike and Sheila, and from his expression, Mike knew Ed had meant for them to overhear his comment. Feeling Sheila stiffen at the insult, Mike held out his hand to the lawyer. "Hello, Ed. Bought any garages lately?"

Julia, who appeared to be holding Frank's elbow as if to steady herself asked, "You're buying garages, Ed? Whatever for?" Her speech was already beginning to slur from the champagne, and the evening had barely begun.

Gail, who had also overheard Ed's derogatory remark and Mike's retort, quickly spoke up. "Ed's not buying a garage. Mike was just joking with him. Don't you remember? Mike owns a garage here in town."

"Really! I've never known anyone before who invested in garages. Is there any money in it?" Julia spewed out melodramatically.

Mike looked the woman straight in the eye. "I'm not an investor. I'm a mechanic." He wanted to continue by saying that he actually got his hands greasy, but stopped himself. Trading insults with a drunk was never worth the effort.

Nervously Gail added, "Yes, Julia. Mike's a mechanic. Isn't that...quaint? I mean...it must be very rewarding work, Mike."

Sheila couldn't believe what she was hearing. She knew Gail had told Julia what Mike did for a living, and she was intentionally trying to embarrass him. The fact that she was probably so drunk that she wouldn't remember the incident tomorrow was of little comfort. And what was Gail doing by referring to Mike's work as quaint and rewarding?

Piqued by her friends' infuriating behavior, Sheila turned to Estelle, knowing that her sister-in-law was capable of even worse than Julia. In a deliberate move to take the offense with Estelle, Sheila said, "I'm glad to see you and Ed have come to wish us well. But I'm frankly surprised that you did."

"Nonsense, Sheila," Estelle replied with hint of agitation in her voice. "Would we miss your party?" Estelle seemed determined to present the picture of a unified family to the world.

"Then you'll come to the wedding as well?" Sheila asked. "We've set the date for April twelfth."

"So soon? That's less than a month away," Estelle protested.

"We could see no reason to wait." Sheila reached for Mike's hand as she searched his eyes for reassurance that he wasn't angry with her for what these people were doing. Mike's frown broke into a smile for Sheila alone, and he squeezed her hand tightly, coaxing a smile back.

"Isn't love marvelous?" Julia sighed dramatically, putting her hand on Frank's chest for support. "I adore being in love." Sotto voce, she informed Sheila, "And if it doesn't work out, you can always divorce him."

Sheila drew away in disgust.

In a firm tone Mike announced, "It's been an interesting party, Gail, but we have to be going." Everyone around looked at him in surprise, but no one protested, not even Gail. He put his arm around Sheila and began to pivot her toward the door. "It's been nice meeting all of you."

Sheila threaded her way behind him through the crowd, holding his hand tightly.

He took his coat and hers from the maid and helped Sheila pull hers on before shrugging into his. "I'm sorry to cut it short, but I felt that it was time for us to go." Mike wasn't sure how Sheila was going to react if he admitted his true feelings about her friends, so he said no more as he helped her into his car.

When she remained silent as he drove them away from Gail's house, he said, "I'm sorry if leaving early like that spoiled your evening."

"No, no. It's not that. I just can't believe this happened. No, I guess I can believe it. That's why I'm so upset. There have been other times during this past year or so that I've wondered how good my relationship was with those people, but I told myself I was imagining things. I'm the one who's sorry for getting you into such an awkward situation."

"It wasn't your fault."

Sheila was quiet for several blocks as her rare anger seethed, then finally surfaced with a loud, "Damn them! How could they do this to me!"

Mike glanced at her in surprise.

"They all knew this was our engagement party." Sheila was close to tears. "Why would they do this?"

Mike took her hand and held it comfortingly. "It might have been a reaction against me."

Sheila wanted to deny it, but she knew he was right. Even her best friend was against her marrying Mike. In retrospect she was sure Gail must have told Julia that Sheila was marrying a man most would consider inappropriate. Julia would have chosen this way to show Sheila that Mike wouldn't fit in with their crowd. "I think it was against both of us. I may have married into the Danforth family, but George is dead now and once more I'm an outsider in this town. A social outcast."

"Do you mind?"

"I can get used to it." She turned to face him. "I saw them with new eyes tonight. You're right about them. They're shallow and uncaring. No friend would put me in a position where I would feel so uncomfortable."

Mike's heart went out to her in sympathy. "At least we still have my friends. They may drink beer rather than champagne, but they'll treat both of us with respect and consideration. They're all good people."

Sheila managed a tremulous smile. "I'm looking forward to meeting them. It seems I now have room for a lot of new friends."

"They will all love you," Mike said confidently. "You can count on it."

Chapter Eleven

When he left Sheila at her house, the night was still young and Mike was in no mood to be alone. If he had been at Gail's party alone, he would have stayed and taken those people to task for their insults, but he knew that to do so in front of Sheila would surely have embarrassed her. As it turned out, he had probably embarrassed her anyway, but he couldn't stand seeing them put her in such an awkward position.

Possibly her friends had ridiculed her for her choice in a husband before they had even met him. He could never hope to fit in with that crowd. If he had worn a sport coat instead of jeans, the evening might have gone better, but he doubted it. Even their conversation was alien to him, but that wasn't Sheila's fault. That was her turf, and the rules were different. He should have known.

All his life Mike had struggled to lift himself above his station. College had been denied him, but he had read until he was better educated than many men with college degrees. He had never made much money, but he owned his garage and all his equipment outright, his cars were paid for, and he had only a house payment. He was still young enough to have hopes of that really big break that comes along once in every life. Tonight, for the first time in years, Mike felt like a failure.

At the moment Sheila was angry with her friends, but he was fairly certain she would give them another chance. Especially Gail. Friends were too important to discard without trying to work out differences. However, they weren't his friends, and he wasn't sure they ever could be. He, too, thought Sheila had been set up as a target for ridicule.

As he often did when he was despondent, Mike headed for Joe's Place, his favorite hangout after the Quick Stop. The bar was owned by Joe Hutchins, a friend from Mike's boyhood. He and Joe had seen each other through a lot of rough times, and they had solved the world's problems more than once over Joe's scarred bar top.

From the large number of cars in the parking lot, Mike surmised that the place was busy. He welcomed the distraction. He was still a bit hurt that Sheila hadn't asked him to stay when he had taken her home, and he was trying hard not to speculate as to why she hadn't wanted him with her. Didn't all women want their men around when they were feeling low? The answer was apparent.

When he entered the dimly lit bar, he was greeted by several of the men and women. These people were his friends. Their easy camaraderie gave him a warm feeling inside. There was nothing phony about these people. If they liked you, you were accepted with no reservation.

He straddled a bar stool and called out a greeting to Joe, who responded in his usual ribald manner. "What's going down, Joe?" Mike replied with a grin. Their initial exchange was as habitual as breathing.

"Same as always. Dorothy has a bee in her bonnet for a new car. You don't have any idea where I can get a good deal, do you?"

"Try Flynn's over in Mapleton. I think he'll be square with you. How's Dorothy doing?"

"Complaining as always, so I guess she's happy."

"You two ought to get married so she can make an honest man out of you."

"Hell, no. Once was enough for me. I ain't never getting married again. Turns out that baby wasn't even mine."

"Well, it wasn't from a lack of trying. What ever happened to Louise, anyway?"

"She took up with that trucker that used to come by here in that fancy maroon Mack truck. That big man with the tattoo of a boat on his arm."

"I remember him. I wondered why he hasn't been in."

"I wish he would. I'd like to buy him a drink. The best day of my life was when Louise took off with him."

Mike asked for a beer and leaned his forearms on the bar. "I've got somebody I want you to meet."

"Not a woman! Look out!"

"Not just any woman. This one's special."

"They all are." Joe cocked his head to one side. "You're really serious, aren't you?"

"I'm going to marry her."

"Damn! Can't you be taught anything? You saw how Louise changed after we got married. Before then she never raised her voice, and afterwards she never lowered it."

"At least she was consistent. No, Sheila's different."

"Sheila?"

"Sheila Danforth."

"Did I hear you say Danforth?"

"That's right."

"Well, I guess you know what the hell you're doing. I wish you all the best if this is really what you want."

"It is. I'm going to bring her in here to meet everybody tomorrow night."

"That's a good time. It's always full to the rafters on a Saturday night. She can meet all your friends at once."

"You're going to like her, Joe. She's a real lady."

Joe grinned and shook his head. "They all are before you marry them."

"Keep talking," Mike said, grinning. "You'll convince yourself one of these days." He downed a large portion of the cold beer.

Yes, these were his friends. The salt of the earth. Sheila would like them so well that she wouldn't care if that stuck-up bunch of society snobs wrote her off. He smiled comfortably at the thought of how well Sheila and his buddies would get along.

* * *

"Are the rings ready yet for Barlow and Danforth?" Sheila asked the lady behind the jewelry counter.

"I believe they are." The woman ran her plump, bejeweled finger down the row of slots. "Here they are." She peered inside the two velvet boxes and smiled. "Wedding rings. How nice!"

Sheila smiled and glanced up at Mike. "The wedding is next month."

Mike grinned down at her with the expression of a man very much in love. "This is the future Mrs. Barlow."

"Isn't that nice?" the motherly woman sighed. "It does me good to see two young people so much in love. And you're wise to have waited until you're old enough to know what you're doing. I see kids fresh out of high school in here every day. They'll be starting families, and they're just children themselves!" She frowned as if she took this problem very much to heart.

"Could we see the rings?" Sheila prompted.

"By all means. Be sure everything is spelled right." She gave Mike's ring to Sheila and hers to him.

Sheila read the inscription in the bright metal and smiled. *Our Rainbow Forever*. Whenever she thought of their love she was reminded of the glistening rainbow they had seen hovering over the falls that snowy morning. The falls had been so fierce and powerful, yet the rainbow hovered just at the precipice in opalescent splendor. It seemed to symbolize their love in the headlong rush of life. She wondered if Mike would remember it.

"Let me see mine," she said.

"No, no!" the woman objected. "It's bad luck for a bride to try on her wedding ring."

"I only want to read the inscription."

"The card says these inscriptions were given privately," she said doubtfully.

"Maybe you'd better wait," Mike agreed in mock seriousness.

"If I can't see mine, then you can't see yours," Sheila bartered with him.

"Come on, just one peep? Just show me the inscription."

"Nope. Not unless I can see mine first."

Mike shook his head in resignation. "If you're going to be that way." He held out the blue velvet box.

Ignoring the salesclerk's disapproving expression, Sheila gave him his ring. Together they held the bands up and read the inscriptions.

"It says the same thing!" Sheila said in surprise.

"How did you know this was what I planned to put in yours?"

"I guess our minds just run along the same track," Sheila replied. "Then you do remember the rainbow?"

"Of course. It's our rainbow."

"I still say you shouldn't have looked," the woman objected. "Everybody knows it's bad luck."

Mike put his arm around Sheila as he handed the woman the rings so she could box them. "With this lady by my side, I can't have anything but good luck."

Sheila smiled happily and took the bag containing the rings when the woman held it out. She felt the same way about Mike. Together they could conquer anything.

Instead of walking back to the car, Mike led her down the sidewalk. "It's getting late. Okay if we eat here?"

"Where?"

"I know a place."

He took her around the corner and down a narrow, picturesque alley that seemed to have a quaint charm all its own. She'd driven by the entrance to this alley numerous times, but had never walked down it before. The pavement was aged brick as were the walls of the buildings. Over the years some of the brick had been painted with advertising signs, most of which had long since faded almost into oblivion. At the end of the short alley was a small green neon sign over a doorway that spelled out, Luigi's.

Inside they were greeted by a short, dark man behind the counter in the open kitchen. He was busy kneading pasta dough, but he called Mike by name and nodded to Sheila. Mike waved to the waitress who was evidently Luigi's wife, and she waved back as she hurried over to take someone's order. There were only six tables, and Mike guided Sheila to one beside a large poster of Corsica.

"I love this place!" Sheila exclaimed as the waitress called out the order to her husband in her native tongue. "How did you ever find it?"

"I saw the sign one night and came back here to see what it was. Luigi and Marta's son owns the clothing store that fronts this place on Main Street. He didn't need the extra space, so Luigi opened a cafe here. Order anything—it's all good."

When the woman named Marta came to their table, she wagged her finger disapprovingly at Mike. "You haven't been in lately. Shame on you. You're wasting away!"

"Marta, this is Sheila, my fiancée."

Marta grinned and folded her hands over her rotund middle. "Fiancée! Luigi! Did you hear Mike?" She rattled off a quick exchange, and Luigi laughed and called out his congratulations.

"Do you have fettuccine today?" Mike asked.

"No, Luigi was lazy this morning. Only made half enough, and we sold it all by lunch." She commented loudly in Italian on her husband's lack of forethought and threw up her hands. Her husband responded in kind. "We have lasagna. Get that instead. It's very good." She leaned closer. "Today his fettuccine was a bit heavy. Be glad it's gone. You want a salad?"

Sheila nodded along with Mike. "What kind of dressing do you have?"

"Get the house dressing. I make it special." Marta turned away and called out the order to Luigi.

"That's one of the things I like about this place," Mike told her as Marta waddled away. "It's almost like eating with the family. Everything is made fresh that day, and when it's gone, it's gone. Or if Luigi doesn't feel like making a particular dish, he doesn't do it. If you want a dessert you have to get here early. They sell out fast."

"You fascinate me. I could have sworn I knew all there was to know about Falls River and Mapleton. You're showing me a whole new side of them both."

"Wait until you see what I have in mind for tonight," he said confidently. "We're going to meet my friends."

"We are?" She glanced down at her clothes. She was wearing a bulky knit sweater in a shade of rich cream over wine-colored slacks. It was an expensive outfit but very casual. "I'm not dressed to meet anyone."

"Sure you are. We're only going to Joe's Place. Nobody will be dressed up."

"If you're sure," she said doubtfully. She would never have dressed like this to meet any of George's friends.

The food was as delicious as Mike had promised, and by the time they ate dessert Sheila felt stuffed. "We can't come here often," she told Mike as they walked back to his car, hand in hand. "If we do, you'll have to roll me home."

In the gathering dusk, he regarded her in the lights from the store windows. "You really like my world, don't you?" he marveled. "At first I was afraid that you wouldn't."

"I love your world. Mike, let's move to Mapleton."

"You're thinking about that house again. You know we decided against it."

"No, I wasn't. I just like Mapleton better than Falls River. We come over here on almost all our dates. Why not live here?"

"It's not that easy. There are already several garages here in Mapleton—as you know—and competition in this type of business is pretty fierce. I have my regular customers in Falls River, and they wouldn't want to drive all the way over here any more than I would want to have to drive to Falls River every day to work."

She shook her finger at him in imitation of Marta. "I have my car repairs done in the local shop these days."

"You'd better," he threatened playfully.

"What are your friends like?" she asked, abruptly changing the subject.

"I guess they're a lot like me. I can promise you this—they are all a far cry from Julia Overton."

"So I gathered. Maybe I was too harsh on my friends last night. Gail called this morning and acted as if nothing happened."

"Did she apologize for putting you in an awkward situation?"

"I don't think she realized I felt awkward."

Mike made no comment.

"After you left last night, I wished I had asked you to stay. Always before I've wanted to be alone when I felt sad or out of sorts. But when you left I felt worse than ever. That house is so lonely. Speaking of houses, are you moving to my house after we're married or am I moving to yours?"

"Which would you prefer?"

"Yours," she answered promptly. "I'll call a realtor tomorrow and put that museum on the market."

"What about all your furniture and things?"

Sheila smiled up at him. "I guess I'll have a whopper of a yard sale. I've always wanted to do that."

Mike chuckled softly at the idea of selling such expensive items out on her lawn. "In your neighborhood it might do well, but hiring an auctioneer might be mandatory."

"There you go again." She poked him playfully. "I'm looking forward to being your wife, even if you are prejudiced."

"You're something else, lady," Mike returned happily. "But I'm not sure what." He dodged as she aimed her blow at his ribs.

They left Mapleton and drove back to Falls River. Joe's Place was on the highway on the south side of town. It was a squatty wooden building with an open pavilion out back where his customers could sit in warmer weather and enjoy the view of the river. The water was black and forbidding in the crisp night air, so Sheila and Mike hurried across the deck to the warmth of the brown building.

"Hi, Joe. What's going down?" Mike called out habitually to the bartender as they entered.

When Joe made his typically ribald reply, Sheila felt Mike tense against her side as his steps faltered for an instant. The bartender's greeting was off-color, but she didn't take offense. She smiled at Mike, and they continued on to the bar.

"Sheila, this is Joe Hutchins. We went to school together. Joe, this is Sheila Danforth. She's the lady I was telling you about."

Joe leaned his brawny forearms on the scuffed bar. "So you're the one that trapped old Mike, are you? Well, Mike, I'll give you this—you fell for pretty bait."

Sheila's smiled wavered, but she decided Joe meant the remark to be complimentary. "It's nice to meet you."

"Hey, Arlo! Come over here and meet Mike's girl!" Joe yelled over the sound of the jukebox and the clatter of two men shooting pool.

"Arlo's here?" Mike asked with some trepidation.

"He rolled in about an hour ago."

"Arlo?" Sheila asked.

"Arlo Wade. He drives a truck for Danforth Furniture on this end of the route and hauls chemicals back."

Whatever else Mike might have been saying was broken off as a huge bear of a man slapped him across the back and crushed his hand in a shake. "Mike! Boy, it's good to see you. What's this about you having a girlfriend?"

Sheila's eyes traveled up the huge man's beer belly, his muscled-padded shoulders, barrel neck, ginger whiskers, and stopped at his small blue eyes. Her mouth had fallen open so she shut it. "I'm Sheila Danforth," she volunteered.

"Sheila," Arlo said, not catching her last name in the noise of the bar. "That's real pretty. You want to dance?"

"She's with me, Arlo," Mike said firmly. "I didn't expect you to be here tonight."

"Yeah, I just pulled in not too long ago. I'm telling you those damned Danforths are driving my rig into the ground. Wouldn't even give me time to rest on the other end." He gave a colorful suggestion as to how the Danforths might occupy their spare time as far as he was concerned.

Mike glanced at Sheila, who was looking rather stunned. "Clean up your act, Arlo. This is the woman I'm going to marry."

"Marry!" Arlo spat out the word as if it were obscene. "Hell, don't do that!"

"I've already tried to talk him out of it," Joe put in. "He won't listen." He winked at Sheila to let her know he was mostly teasing.

Arlo, who had spent the past several hours drinking away his paycheck, shook his massive head dolefully. "Think about it, Mike. Marriage!" He described wedded bliss in terms that made Sheila blink in surprise.

"Hey," Mike said in a deceptively easy tone. "I know you've been drinking, but watch it. Okay?"

The big man hid a belch behind his fist. "Sorry, Sheila," he said contritely. "I didn't mean nothing."

Mike looked around the smoky room, and with relief recognized the couple in the far booth. "Come on, honey. I want you to meet these people."

Sheila followed him to the booth. The woman's eyes lit up at the sight of Mike, but her expression cooled when she saw Sheila, and her gaze appraised Sheila's clothing, fur parka and hairstyle. Mike slid into the opposite seat, and Sheila had no choice but to scoot in after him.

"Sheila, this is Bill and Euba Swartz. This is my fiancée, Sheila Danforth."

The man grinned. "I didn't know you were getting married. Congratulations."

"I haven't seen you around Joe's," Euba said to Sheila. "Are you new in town?"

"No, I've just never been to Joe's before. I've been to the Quick Stop though."

"Is Sam still selling goat meat out there?" Bill asked.

"Goat?" Sheila rose to the bait.

"He's kidding," Mike told her. "How are the kids, Euba?"

"Driving me crazy." She lit a cigarette and blew the smoke upward. "Bill here gets to escape when he goes to work, but with nobody hiring these days I'm stuck at home." To Sheila she held up four fingers. "I've got four. The youngest is still in diapers, but the biggest one is finally in school this year. They keep you busy." She tapped her cigarette in the direction of the ashtray. So far she hadn't smiled at all.

"Bill, what kind of work are you in?" Sheila asked.

"You mean what do I do for a living? I run a backhoe."

"Euba," Mike said, "could you give Sheila the recipe for that pie you made when I was over there last? I think it was the best you ever baked."

Euba's thin lips curved slightly in the expectancy of a smile, but never quite made it. "I'd be glad to, but it's expensive to make. All that sugar and butter and eggs. Of course I use margarine, but it's still something you'll just want to cook for company. Especially since you two are just starting out. After a while you'll learn to cut corners. We all do."

Sheila held her tongue and wondered if Mike expected her to be close friends with this woman. They had nothing at all in common, though Euba was pleasant enough. Euba launched into a quick recital of the pie's ingredients that sailed right over Sheila's head. Because she so rarely cooked, Sheila had no retention for recipes and even less interest. But since Mike seemed to have enjoyed the pie so much, she felt she ought to get the recipe for Marie. In a flash it occurred to her that she would likely not have Marie to cook for them. She would be doing all that herself. She had to admit that she wasn't very good at it, but that was probably because she had had so little practice. She would enjoy cooking for Mike, she assured herself—once she learned how. As the woman continued to rattle off the instructions, Sheila interrupted her. "I'm sorry. Would you mind writing that down for me? I've already forgotten the first things you said, and I'll never remember the amounts."

"It's pretty much a basic cheese pie except for the coconut."

"I'm not much of a cook, I'm afraid." She heard Mike and Bill talking about something that sounded far more interesting than recipes, but Euba showed no inclination to join the other conversation.

"You'll learn to cook quick enough. This must be your first marriage."

"No, actually I—"

Before she could finish, Arlo Wade swaggered up. "Hello, Bill!" he bellowed. "What are you doing hiding over here in the corner? I nearly didn't see you. Hi, Euba. How's them little brats?"

"Just awful."

Arlo put his palms down between the paper place mats and leaned all his weight on the table. Sheila hoped it was stronger than it looked. "Bill, is your company hiring?" he asked with the exaggerated seriousness of a drunk.

"No, and even if they were, we don't hire on truckers. I work for a construction company."

"Damn. I've just got to get loose from that blood-sucking furniture company. They're running me ragged."

Mike nudged Sheila. "I think we'd better be going."

They slid out of the booth, but instead of following Mike, Sheila lagged behind. As she gazed up at Arlo, she asked, "Why are you so upset with the furniture company?"

Arlo sighed morosely and suggested an improbable ancestry of the Danforth family. "They sit up there in their fancy houses and look down on us working men. You'd never see a Danforth in a place like Joe's. They aren't good, common people. They're snobs. Every one of them. And not only that..." He finished with a description that implied an unusual family closeness.

When Mike realized that Sheila was not behind him, he quickly returned for her. As he neared, he heard Arlo's last comment. Clenching his fists at his side, he said tersely, "Let's go, Sheila."

Instead, she continued to glare up at Arlo. "*I'm* a Danforth. And I'm here in Joe's Place. And *I'm* not—"

"Sheila!" Mike could barely contain himself.

"You're a what?" Arlo roared. "A Danforth! What the hell do you think you're doing here in our place! Get back across the river where you belong!" He made a sweeping gesture that was probably meant for emphasis, but the beer had so affected his coordination that he bumped Sheila's mouth with the back of his hand. She wasn't hurt, but she cried out in surprise.

Mike's reaction was both automatic and effective. One hard fist buried itself in Arlo's paunch, the other caught Arlo on the jaw as the huge man doubled over. Arlo fell to the floor like a beached whale.

"Mike! You hit him! What—"

Bill cut in, "He's coming to!"

Mike grabbed Sheila's arm and pulled her toward the door. "Run like hell. I'll explain to Arlo when he's sober."

As they ran to Mike's car, Sheila heard a bull-like bellow that meant Arlo was awake and was not amused. She threw herself into Mike's side of the car and scrambled over as Arlo stumbled out the doorway of Joe's Place. He growled again and was about to come after Mike when Joe and Bill grabbed him and tried to pull him back. Arlow's forward progress was slowed but not stopped as he continued across the lot, dragging the two men with him.

"What will he do if he catches us?" Sheila asked as Mike spun out of the parking lot.

"I don't know. Nobody has ever been stupid enough to hit Arlo before."

"Then why did you?"

"Because he hit you!"

"It was an accident!"

"He still hit you!"

A smile tilted Sheila's lips, and a laugh bubbled up from her throat. Mike glanced at her and frowned. "What's so funny?"

"All of it." She laughed.

In spite of himself, Mike grinned. "Arlo did look pretty strange wearing Joe and Bill as sleeves, didn't he?"

Sheila slouched down in the seat and tried to smother her giggles before they erupted into hysteria. "I've never been in a barroom brawl before."

"Stick with me, baby, and I'll show you the world." Mike flexed his right hand experimentally. It was stinging all the way to his elbow, but it didn't seem to be broken. When he parked in Sheila's driveway, he looked at her closely. "Your lip is swelling."

"So is your hand. Come inside and I'll fix us some ice packs."

She took him to the kitchen and wrapped a handful of ice cubes in a damp dishcloth for each of them. As Mike gingerly touched his to his knuckles and Sheila applied hers to her mouth, she burst out laughing again. "We certainly look as if we had a fun date."

"At least there was no one like Julia Overton in the place. That's all I promised," he reminded her with a laugh.

"You know something? I don't like your friends any better than you like mine!" For some reason Sheila's observation struck them both as funny.

"You know what? Neither do I."

"You sure decked that big bully."

Mike grinned. "I did, didn't I?"

"Do something for me. Don't ever show me a good time again, okay? I'm not in shape for it."

Mike put his arms around her and kissed the side of her mouth that wasn't sore. "Are you sure you aren't hurt?"

"It surprised me more than anything. I bit myself. See?" She showed him the pink crescent inside her lip. "He barely touched me. Really."

"I'll bet you never had this much fun with any of your other dates."

"I can honestly say that tonight has been unique," she answered, struggling to keep a straight face and failing.

As he held her, he grew serious. "There's no way you're going to fit into my world, are you?"

"It's going to be about as easy as fitting you into mine." She nestled her cheek against his chest. "I guess we'll have to find a world of our own."

"I guess so. After tonight I'm not so sure I still want my old one. I never noticed how rough they are. Joe has always had a raunchy mouth, but tonight I really heard what he was saying."

"Joe wasn't nearly as bad as Arlo."

"No, but I don't consider Arlo as one of my friends. He's like the five-hundred-pound gorilla in the joke— he sits anywhere he wants to."

"There's one good thing about it."

"What's that?"

"Arlo doesn't know where I live. You can hide out here until the heat's off, kid," she said in a terrible impression of a gangster in an old-time movie.

"Can I hide under your bed?" he suggested with a hopeful leer.

"Play your cards right and I'll let you hide *in* my bed."

"I can't beat a deal like that." Mike put his arm around her, and she wrapped hers around his waist. Together they went upstairs.

Chapter Twelve

Sheila," Estelle said in a pitying voice, "I can't bear to see you make such a terrible mistake."

"What mistake?" Sheila asked as she perched on the arm of the sofa, hoping Estelle would take the hint and leave soon.

"You know exactly what I mean. Marrying this Mike Barlow. He isn't our sort at all."

"I know," she replied with a cryptic smile. "He isn't."

"Surely you must know about his reputation. Ed says Mike has actually been arrested! For disturbing the peace!"

"How does Ed know about that? Have you been checking up on him? I already know about that, and I also know there were extenuating circumstances."

"You can't possibly marry someone with a criminal record!"

"Don't be silly, Estelle. Mike doesn't have a criminal record. He just had to pay a fine. Besides, I'm a good influence on him." Sheila recalled seeing Arlo Wade lying flat on his back in the barroom and had to hide her smile. Estelle would never understand.

"Sheila," Estelle said as if she were trying hard to reason with a simpleminded person. "Please reconsider before you make a tragic mistake. Mark my words, if you marry this man, you'll be divorced within the year."

"No, I won't."

"Can't you see that he's only after your money?"

Sheila stood up abruptly. "That's enough, Estelle. I have other things I need to be doing. You'll have to go."

Estelle's flat cheeks paled with suppressed anger, and she said stiffly, "If that's what you want. But mark my words, I'm not at all sure you'll be accepted here as Mike's wife. You may have already ruined your social future."

"Goodbye, Estelle."

Sheila saw the woman out and closed the front door firmly. Her mind was in a turmoil. Everyone was so positive she was making a mistake, yet she was equally certain that she wasn't. Even her maid was still haughtily reserved. When Marie had changed the sheets that morning, she had snapped them in the air over the bed in an obvious pique of temper.

No sooner had Estelle driven away than Marie came to Sheila. "Mrs. Danforth?"

"Yes?"

"I'm giving my notice."

"You're what?" Sheila wondered if the maid had been eavesdropping on her conversation with Estelle. She was reminded of rats deserting a sinking ship.

"When I came to work for you, I agreed to give you two weeks' notice before I quit."

Sheila drew a steady breath. "Are you certain you want to do this? I doubt you could find better wages anywhere else in the area."

"Yes, ma'am. I'm sure." Marie's expression was implacable.

"I see. Very well. I accept your notice, and I'll start looking for a replacement right away."

"Will you give me a recommendation?"

After a pause, Sheila said, "Yes. I've had no complaints about your work. Your attitude is a different matter, but that's between you and your next employer."

Marie looked miffed, but held her tongue. Sheila walked past her and up to her room. She knew a replacement of Marie's caliber wouldn't be easy to find in Falls River. Then she remembered that when she married Mike in a few weeks and moved into his small house, she would have to let Marie go anyway. In the excitement of her growing love for Mike, she had managed to shelve that particular detail. Or had she unconsciously set it aside because she hadn't wanted to think about it? Not once in her life had she lived in a house without a maid. She decided that was absurd. During the weeks after Marie's last day, she could manage the huge house by herself.

She dialed Mike's number, and when he answered she said, "Can you take the day off tomorrow?"

"I guess I can. We aren't very busy right now. Why?"

"I need to get away and I want to be with you."

"Sure. Carl can do anything that's likely to come up around here. What do you have in mind?"

"I have a summer house on Leetes Island, just up the coast from New Haven. We'd have the beach to ourselves."

"A summer house and private beach?" Mike's voice sounded strained again.

Sheila tried to mask her defensiveness. "No, it's not a private beach exactly, but this time of the year most of the houses around there are vacant."

"Sure. That'll be fine with me. When do you want to go?"

"Can we leave when you get off work today?"

"I'll pick you up at five. I'd better get off the phone now. A customer just drove up."

Sheila said goodbye and hung up. Maybe it was just her jangled nerves that were making her so suspicious of his voice inflections. After packing her overnight bag, she tried to read as she waited for the hands of the clock to creep to five.

Sheila heard Marie leave on the hour. All round her the house's oppressive silence crowded in on her, and she frowned at how alien she felt in her own home. She should have sold it right after George's death. From her window she saw the realtor she had contacted placing a sign on the broad lawn. It couldn't sell fast enough to suit her.

Mike was a few minutes late, and when he arrived Sheila was waiting for him with packed bags. As always when she saw his welcoming grin, she felt a surge of love. She put her arms around him and hugged him as he kissed her neck. In Mike's embrace all her troubles seemed smaller.

They drove out of town and headed toward the coast, talking about the minor events of the day. Sheila felt herself relaxing and hoped it would always be like this between them. With Mike beside her, she felt so secure and free.

They reached the coast before dark and turned onto the highway that led to Leetes Island. At intervals the sea, flat and glistening like pewter, could be seen between the rows of houses. The farther out they drove, the larger were the cottages and the more impressive their entrance gates.

Mike glanced at the houses and wondered if they were nearing Sheila's beach house. The homes they were passing looked large enough to be year-round residences. He reached over and took her hand. She smiled at him.

Watching for familiar landmarks in the dusk, Sheila pointed ahead. "Turn in the next drive."

Mike drove between twin brick columns and down a graveled drive. Ahead stood a two-story house with the sturdy elegance of a Cape-Cod-style home. He looked to either side for a beach house and headed for the smaller building he saw behind the garage.

"Where are you going? You drove past the house."

Mike slowed to a stop and looked back at the large structure. "That's it? That's a beach house?"

"Back up. The caretaker will put the car away."

"Caretaker?"

"He and his wife live in the cottage there. We'll have the house to ourselves."

Mike didn't comment. He didn't dare. This beach house of hers was twice the size of his home—the one that was soon to become her home as well. He didn't know how he would ever be able to accept her wealth. And he still worried that in time she might come to resent his lack of it.

An elderly man with wispy white hair came out to meet them, and Sheila greeted him warmly. "Mike, this is my caretaker, Joseph Beam. Joseph, this is my fiancé, Mike Barlow. We're to be married next month."

"Glad to meet you," the man said with a nod to Mike. The man had their suitcases in hand before Mike could get to them. He was old enough to be Mike's grandfather, and Mike felt very awkward watching him carry the heavy bags. But there was nothing he could do short of pulling them out of the man's hands. "Heda has supper cooking. She said it would be done by eight o'clock."

"How is Heda?" Sheila asked as she followed Joseph up onto the porch.

"As well as can be. The winter settles in her bones, you know."

"You ought to move inland, though I don't know how I could ever replace you."

"And leave Leetes Island? No, I grew up here, same as Heda. We'll stay here. I wouldn't be comfortable if I couldn't be near the sea."

The house was cozy inside, with polished oak flooring and braided rugs beneath the overstuffed chintz-covered sofa and chairs in the living room. A fire crackled in the wide fireplace, and the mantel served as a shelf for a model of a high-masted schooner. Several pictures of wildflowers and sea gulls hung on the pale rose walls. Through the wide doorway, Mike could see the dining room and an oak cupboard with blue willow dishes.

"Nice place," he said, hoping his comment sounded genuine, as Joseph left to carry their bags upstairs.

"I like it. For a while after George died, I considered living here, but during the winter the beach is almost deserted. I was afraid I'd be too lonely."

Mike pulled open the curtain and gazed across the open porch to the sea. "I think I would be less lonely here than in your museum."

"I'd like to keep this place after we're married. I know you may feel it's ostentatious, but there's Heda and Joseph to think of. Marie can find work elsewhere—in fact she gave me her two-weeks' notice today—but the Beams are too old to start all over."

"I understand."

"You don't think I'm foolish to keep a house so my caretakers will have something to do?"

"It's not foolish," he tried to reassure her. "I think that's a very nice thing to do for them." Uncomfortable with the subject, Mike asked, "Why is Marie quitting?"

Sheila turned away. "She probably thinks she can find a better position."

"And she doesn't want to work for the wife of a garage mechanic?" As soon as the words were out, Mike regretted the way he had responded.

"We won't need a maid in your house. I'll take care of it myself."

"What about all the things you do now? The clubs and the teas. That sort of thing?"

She shrugged and pretended to examine a seashell that she had picked up from a side table. "I've decided to drop out of the women's clubs," she said lightly. "They take up too much time."

"Sheila?"

"All right. So they have some rather stringent requirements for membership. I've gotten bored with them. I really have. I would probably drop out of them anyway."

Mike turned back to watch the waves roll to the shore. He knew exactly why she was dropping out of the clubs.

"Would you like to take a walk on the beach? It will be dark soon so we should leave now if we want to see anything."

"Sure." He opened the back door for her and looped his arm companionably over her shoulders.

The brisk air lightly salted his lips as they walked down the weathered steps to the beach. Overhead, a couple of birds circled, hoping for a handout, and when none was offered they flew away. Waves reared high offshore, raced toward the beach and toppled over to foam on the tan shore. Behind Mike and Sheila, their footprints trailed in a zigzag line in the sand.

"A storm must be building out there," Sheila commented as she looked out to sea. "The waves aren't usually this big."

"Do you come here often?"

"Not as often as I would like." After a few minutes of silence, she said. "I don't suppose you would consider moving here?"

"My line of work would hardly be welcome in this neighborhood. And I certainly couldn't commute."

"I didn't think you would."

"I had to deliver a car to Mapleton today, and I drove by that house. It's still for sale."

Sheila made no comment. She knew it was still on the market because she had called to ask. "Maybe I should get a job."

"I shouldn't have mentioned it."

They walked arm in arm in silence. Ahead of them the sun was lowering over the mainland. The sky slowly brightened to a lilac pink and then to vivid hues of rose and gold. Long clouds hung like streaks of molten lava above the swollen orange globe.

"I love this time of day," Sheila murmured. "I can lay everything aside and mellow out."

"I like it, too. Look out there. The sea is turning purple."

Beyond the waves the water was darkening with the sky above. In contrast, the froth of the waves was almost translucent. The chilly breeze off the water was becoming colder.

"We had better head back," Sheila said. "The beach can get awfully dark, and I didn't think to bring a flashlight."

They turned and retraced their steps. Already the growling waves had obliterated most of their tracks.

"There is something primitive about the sea," Mike said. "I can see how men have always wanted to combat it. Think what it would be like to be on a schooner out there beyond the sight of land. To watch the sun sink beyond the curve of the earth and be surrounded by nothing but night."

"That sounds more frightening than fun. There's a storm out there."

"No, no. It's adventurous."

Sheila laughed. "I guess that's why the men sailed off and the women stayed home. I prefer my adventures in a movie theater or on TV."

"Some people would say you're entering into an adventure by marrying me. How many women really give up all they know to marry a hell-raiser?"

"You're a pretty tame hell-raiser," she objected.

"Tell that to Arlo Wade."

Sheila smiled up at him. "How many women ever have a man really fight for them? Maybe you are an adventure at that."

They paused at the base of the steps that led up to the house. Although the steps were lighted by a series of antique-style lanterns, they did more to enhance the ambience than to dispel the darkness.

"Is something wrong?" Sheila asked as Mike shoved his hands into his pockets and stared up at the house.

"It's just so damned expensive!"

"No, it's paid for."

"That's not what I mean. Look at it, Sheila. Try to see it with my eyes. It's as big as the house in Mapleton that I can't afford—and it's only your beach house!"

Sheila's forehead puckered in concern as she looked from Mike to the house and back again. "It's just a house."

"Yeah," he growled. "*Just* a house."

She had no idea how to respond, so she waited quietly until Mike started up the steps. In her opinion, the main problem was Mike's prejudice against her wealth, and with all the tension they were faced with, she was getting tired of hearing his complaints. If she were poor, he would never make her feel so bad about it. Sheila had never before been the target for prejudice, and she wasn't at all sure how to handle it.

They ate in comparative silence. Heda Beam had worked hard on the meal, and the food was delicious, but Sheila could hardly force herself to eat it. She kept stealing glances at Mike, but he seemed doggedly determined not to meet her eyes.

After dinner, Heda washed up and left for her own cottage. Sheila watched in relief as the older woman crossed the lawn. The effort of pretending nothing was wrong between Mike and herself was exhausting. Turning to face him across the sitting room, Sheila had to break the excruciating silence. "Do you want to talk about it?"

"There's no point in it." His eyes found hers, and he studied her face at length before turning back to inspect the model ship on the mantel.

Sheila felt a sense of foreboding steal over her. "I can't help who I am, Mike."

"I don't want to change who you are. I love you. It's this." He made a sweeping gesture with his hand. "I can't fit into this kind of life."

"I'll fit into yours," she said quickly.

He sighed and ran his finger along the polished rail of the miniature schooner.

Sheila rose to her feet quickly. "Would you like to see the bedroom?"

He followed her up the stairs, and she opened one of three doors. The master bedroom took up the back half of the house. Tall windows opened onto a view of the ocean, now invisible in the night except for the moon-silvered breakers. Heda had turned down the bed, and the room was softly lighted by a bedside lamp.

"Very nice," Mike said.

"Don't sound like that. It *is* nice. Don't hold it against me that I can give you things like this." Sheila tried to keep the desperation from her voice but failed. "I brought you here because I thought you would enjoy it, not to make you feel...whatever it is that you're feeling."

"Intimidated?" he suggested bitterly. "Inadequate?" He strode to the bed and lifted a corner of the fine rose sheet. "I want to be able to give *you* these things! I want to come to you someday and say, 'Here it is,' and give you a fortune. One that *I* made!"

Sheila clasped her hands together. "I love you," she whispered. Her green eyes were round with fright at what he seemed to be leading toward. "I love you, Mike."

He looked long at her, then pulled her to him almost roughly. "I love you, too," he said fiercely, burying his face in her hair. "I love you so damned much that it hurts!"

Sheila clutched him tightly and tried to choke back her tears. She could hear a finality in his voice that she had never heard before. When he knotted his hand in her hair and lifted her face to his, she met his lips with all the passion in her soul.

With practiced fingers Mike removed her clothing as his lips drank again and again from her love. Then he stripped off his own and pulled her down beside him on the wide bed. He leaned over her, the lamp-light gilding his hard flesh. His thick hair fell over his forehead like an unruly golden mane. In contrast, his eyes were dark and almost savage in their intensity. In their brown depths Sheila saw an intense pain that frightened her as much as had his words.

She closed her eyes and reached up to claim his sculpted lips. Mike's hand caressed her slender rib cage and cupped her breasts possessively. At once Sheila felt a surging need to be one with him. To remove as many barriers as was humanly possible. She moved against him, loving the way his flesh was firm and warm against hers. His body was lean and long, and it excited her in spite of her fears for their future. She ran her hand along the hard curve of his back and over the swell of his buttocks. He was her mate, and nothing had ever been so right before in all her life. Surely nothing could take this away from her!

Mike's fingers teased her nipple, and she arched hungrily toward him. Her teeth parted to meet his tongue with hers, and she felt the swirling sensation his kisses and caresses so often evoked. He lowered his head, leaving a fiery trail of kisses down her slender throat and over the curve of her breast. When his lips closed over her nipple and he traced his tongue over the pouting bud, she moaned aloud.

With an intensity she had never experienced before, Mike ignited a white-hot passion. Slipping his arm beneath her waist, he lifted her to his demanding mouth. Sheila laced her fingers in his hair and moaned with desire. He drew his knee up between her legs, and she eagerly opened herself to him. As they became one, he groaned as if it took all his strength to hold himself in check. The knowledge that she was able to excite him so much delighted Sheila even more, and she moved with him in the ageless dance of love.

As his hand teased and urged her nipple to greater tautness, Mike held her close and kissed her with a fervor that stirred her very soul. Sheila felt her senses soar in the unmistakable culmination of their loving. She fought to draw the sensation out, to make it last, but suddenly it burst within her, and she cried out as wave after wave of intense satisfaction pounded through her. Her release triggered his own, and Mike murmured her name as he held her to him in his own fulfillment.

For a long time they seemed to float in the golden afterglow of love. As she lay nestled in his embrace, Sheila felt Mike's strong chest against her cheek and heard the steady rhythm of his heart. For as long as possible she kept her thoughts and fears at bay, but eventually she lifted her head to look at him. He was gazing back at her, his eyes dark and unreadable.

"Mike?" she whispered.

Without speaking, he put his fingertips to her lips to silence her. Threading his fingers through her hair, he pulled her head back down to his shoulder and nuzzled his cheek in her hair. Once again Sheila closed her eyes and tried hard not to think. After a long time, her breathing became deep and measured, and Mike knew that she slept. Still he held her, stroking the dark silk of her hair and breathing the sweet fragrance he always associated with her. He found sleep elusive, but he wouldn't have sought it if it were possible. Not tonight. There might never be another night when he held her in his arms, and he didn't want to miss a minute of it.

That afternoon, before he had come to pick Sheila up, Joe Hutchins had come by the garage. He had teased Mike about marrying money and getting a beauty in the bargain. Mike hadn't let Joe know how the words had stung, but he knew they were only a sample of what he could expect if he married Sheila.

He looked around the room that could have been featured in a magazine. What was he doing in a place like this? He was just Mike Barlow of Barlow's Garage and Towing Service. He didn't fit here. No more than Sheila fit in his aging house with the water-stained ceiling from the obstinate leak in the roof.

He forced himself to look ahead at the years. Right now Sheila loved him with all her heart—he didn't doubt that at all. But how would she feel in ten years? Would the leaky roof and the grease-grimed laundry be too much for her? How could he ask her to give up the life of a princess? He recalled how his mother's hands had always seemed to be red and knotted from hard work, and he compared that memory to Sheila's petal-soft hands.

He flexed the muscles of his jaws as he blinked to keep back the sadness that threatened to overwhelm him. He couldn't do that to Sheila. She was open and giving, and she would fall in love again if he were out of the picture, this time with someone better suited for her. Almost anyone would be better for her, Mike thought angrily. Anyone at all.

He shifted so that he could see the velvet curve of her cheek and the highlights of her sleek hair. Gently he pulled the covers up over her shoulders and kissed her forehead. She snuggled closer to him without ever waking.

With a sigh, Mike accepted his fate. He had loved an angel, an impossible dream. Now it was time to return to reality. Reaching out, he turned off the lamp.

Chapter Thirteen

Mike slept very little that night. By dawn he was exhausted and in a rotten mood. To keep from waking Sheila, he eased himself out of bed and dressed as quietly as possible.

As difficult as it had been for him to decide to leave her, trying to carry through with it in the pale light of day seemed almost impossible. Already his body was aching for her, and he considered crawling back under the covers and searching out her warm, velvety skin. But with a scowl, he resisted the temptation and shrugged into his coat. His yearning for Sheila was an almost irresistible force that he would have to learn to control. Otherwise he would never be able to stay away, and their mutual torture would never end.

He hurried down the stairs, quickly pulled on his coat and let himself out her back door. He had to get some air and maintain his distance from Sheila or he knew his resolve would collapse. The air coming off the sea was frosty but invigorating, and the sky, above the opalescent hues of dawn, was clear. The sea looked as soft and rosy-hued as a watercolor painting and the waves lapped gently against the newly washed beach. The storm that had been brewing offshore must have moved out to sea.

He saw no sign of the caretakers, and assumed they must be unaccustomed to early risers. That was fine with him because he was in no mood to be civil. He went down the steps to the beach and walked out onto the sand left firm from the receding tide. Numerous gulls circled, vying for what food they might find in the wet sand and shallows that had been left behind.

Mike paused and looked back at the house. It was big, all right. No doubt about it. He had rather hoped it would seem less impressive in the morning light. Instead the opposite was true. The house could have been in the Danforth family before Sheila married into it, or it could have been one of George's purchases. That wasn't the point. Mike knew he could never afford to buy such a magnificent house, let alone one like this to use on weekends.

He shoved his hands into his coat pockets and strode off in the direction they had taken the night before. On a sea-silvered log that partially protruded from the sand, Mike sat down to gaze out across the restless water. As much as he loved Sheila, he was too proud to let it be said that he married her for her money. He might not have many things, but he did have his self-respect.

He wondered if he would be feeling the same way if he had the kind of wealth that these people had. Sheila had often called him a snob, and Mike had to admit she might be right. Although he resented feeling that way, the prejudice was there, and he didn't know how to make it go away. If Zachary Danforth had never come to Falls River, it might be the Barlows that lived on Hazelglen.

Sheila awoke with a start, and for an instant couldn't shake off the nightmare she had been having. She had been running toward or from something—she wasn't sure which—and feeling utterly bereft and alone, crying as she ran into the night. Finally catching her breath, she forced herself to be calm as she reached beside her for Mike's reassuring bulk. Her hand found only cool sheets. Quickly she sat up.

At first she was afraid he was gone. Then she remembered they had come in his car, and she felt sure he wouldn't leave her stranded here at the beach house. When she noticed his zippered bag on the chair near the bed, she let out her pent-up breath, realizing he must have just gone downstairs. She lay back and stared up at the ceiling as she examined her thoughts. Never had she been so afraid of losing someone in all her life. Even when George had died, she hadn't felt so despondent as the thought of losing Mike made her feel. He was now so much a part of her life that she ached at the mere thought of being without him.

All her life Sheila had prided herself on being independent. True, until George's accident she had never had the opportunity to live that way; but since then she had proved she was capable of taking care of

herself. Until she met Mike. Now she found herself
feeling very vulnerable and dependent on him. It
wasn't a sensation she especially liked. It was as if for
the first time she had more than she could bear to lose.
Was this the double-edged sword of love—to know the
loss of the one you loved would cut a wound too deep
to heal?

She rolled out of bed, slipped into her robe and
padded barefoot to the window. Although the windows were closed, Sheila could imagine the tang of sea
salt in the air. At the edge of the sand dunes, she saw
Mike sitting on the old submerged log. From the way
he sat, hunched over with his forearms resting on his
knees, he looked troubled. Worry knotted her stom-
ach. She knew Mike very well, despite the short time
they had known each other, and she sensed what he
must be thinking.

Sheila looked around the bedroom, trying to see it
as he must. It had been a mistake to bring him here at
this time; he was having enough trouble with her house
in town. When she had suggested they come here, she
had thought only of the soothing atmosphere of the
beach.

Hurriedly Sheila pulled on a pair of chino slacks
and a fisherman knit sweater. She brushed her hair as
she stepped into her scuffed deck shoes. Outside the
window, she saw Mike stand up and throw a pebble at
the ocean. Not bothering to put on makeup, Sheila ran
down the stairs.

When she met him on the beach, his drawn face told
her she was right about his thoughts. "I woke up and
missed you," she said. "Have you been for a walk?"

"I needed to think." He stopped several feet from her. "We have to talk."

Without reservation, Sheila went to him, and he put his arm around her shoulders as she matched her stride to his. "I know we do," she said.

"You already know what I'm going to say, don't you." He made it a statement, not a question.

"I've been thinking," she said with forced lightness past the lump in her throat. "I could give this beach house to the Beams."

"Give it away?" He sounded as though he found the idea ludicrous. "A whole house?"

Realizing her mistake, Sheila said quickly, "Or better yet, I can deed it over to Estelle. It belonged to her parents before they died. That would be better. I know she will keep the Beams on for as long as they want to live here."

Mike didn't respond as he maintained a determined pace.

"Did I tell you the real estate in Falls River has a possible client in mind for my house? Maybe it will sell quickly and I can move in with you even before the wedding." She held her breath.

"Maybe you ought to take the house off the market."

"Not sell the museum?" She laughed shakily. "What would we do with two houses?"

Again he was silent.

"I really think I should move in early anyway. Once Marie is gone that house will be more like a mausoleum than a museum. I'll move my things over and have her give the house a special cleaning before she leaves. That way it will stay looking nice for the prospective buyers.''

"Sheila, you're making this harder on both of us."

She wanted to continue to talk about their wedding plans, hoping to avoid forever the words she knew he would say, but her mouth had gone suddenly dry, and she couldn't get any words out. She could hardly breathe. Her eyes searched the horizon as if looking for a reprieve.

"It won't work between us. I've tried. You've tried. The gap in our life-styles is just too wide."

"That's nonsense," she managed to say.

"No, it's not."

"Our lives are what we make them. If our present styles don't suit us anymore, we can change them."

"It's not that easy."

"We can buy a house in Falls River. One you feel comfortable in."

"It's not the house, it's us."

"But I love you," she protested. "Have your feelings changed toward me?"

"No."

"Then don't throw this away!"

"I'm all wrong for you. Ask anybody! Sheila, I love you too much to cage you up in a relationship that you'll come to hate."

"Don't talk like that!"

"You don't seem to realize all you'll be giving up. Be reasonable!"

"Are you thinking I'm too old for you?" In spite of his earlier reassurances that the age difference was no longer an issue, she somehow hoped that it still was; it was an easier problem to face. "That's it, isn't it!

You think I'm too old for you or that you're too young for me."

"No! Of course not!"

"Then we can solve this. We couldn't change the age difference, but we can change everything else!"

"No woman in her right mind would give up a fortune in order to marry a poor man. That's crazy!"

"I wasn't going to give it away. We can put the money in a trust or something and leave it to our children."

"Great. Then my kids would be millionaires, too."

"Well, I'll burn the damned money if it will make you happy!"

"And five years from now you'd hate me for it!"

"Don't stand there and tell me how I'll feel in five years." Her voice rose to match his shouting. "You don't know. In five years you may be a millionaire in your own right!"

"No way, lady!"

"It's not a dirty word, Mike!"

He turned away and tried to calm himself. "See? We can't even discuss it."

"That's because you're being unreasonable."

"It's not me who won't listen to reason."

"Do you think a love like ours comes along every day? How can you even suggest we give each other up?"

"I'm doing what I feel is best."

"Best for whom? This isn't best for me, I can tell you that. And I don't think it is for you, either."

"With me out of the way you'll find someone more suitable."

"I want *you*." She came to a stop in front of him and stared into his face. "Don't do this, Mike!"

"I have to." He tenderly reached out and touched the cool softness of her cheek, then regretfully pulled back his hand. "Go get your things together. It's time to leave."

Sheila straightened her back and lifted her chin in a regal gesture. Her heart might be breaking, but she would be damned if she would grovel. Her eyes met his in a level, accusing glare. Without a word, she turned and went back to the house, leaving him on the beach.

Heda Beam was in the kitchen when Sheila entered, and she came to meet her in the dining room. "Will you and Mr. Barlow care for toast or biscuits with your breakfast?"

"Neither, thank you. We won't have time to eat."

"No time?" Heda's hearing wasn't as keen as it once had been, so she cocked her head to one side in a questioning manner.

"I can't explain now. We have to get back to town right away." Sheila kept her voice measured, but she felt tears welling just under the surface. If she said much more, she would break down altogether. Instead, she hurried up the stairs.

Trying not to think, Sheila threw their clothes back into their respective bags. She dropped to her knees to retrieve one of Mike's socks from under the bed, then zipped up his canvas bag. Anger was replacing the devastating hurt, and she found an unexpected comfort in it. She would rather be furious than to feel so splintered inside. How could he be so stupid as to throw their love away just because there were adjustments to be made! Didn't he realize all marriages involved adjustments? Maybe she was better off without him! No, she wasn't angry enough to believe that.

She carried the bags downstairs and again tried to explain to Heda that they were going back to Falls River. By the time she had made Heda understand, Joseph entered the house, and she had to explain it all over again. Something had come up—they had to leave; no, they wouldn't be back that night.

When Mike came in through the back door, Sheila broke off her explanations and glared at him. He, too, seemed to have had time to get good and angry; he glared back. In stony silence Sheila turned and strode out of the house. Mike mumbled a goodbye to the Beams and followed Sheila to the car.

She sat in grim determination on her side of the car, her eyes riveted ahead. Mike slammed his door with unnecessary firmness and started the engine. All the way back to Falls River they kept a rigorous silence.

When Mike pulled up in front of her house, Sheila yanked open her own door and fumbled in her purse for her house keys. She glared at him as she slid out. "You're dead wrong about this, Mike, but I'm not going to crawl. I love you, and this won't change how I feel. You take your foolish pride, and see if it keeps you warm at night. If you ever change your mind, I'll be waiting." She slammed the car door as hard as she could and stepped back as he peeled out of the portico and spun down the drive.

Grumbling under her breath, Sheila unlocked her door and tossed her bag and purse inside. Stamping out toward the street, she grabbed the real estate sign and yanked it out of the ground. She went back to the house, carrying it like a club, and tossed it across the drive. There was no point in selling the house if she didn't have somewhere else to go.

Once inside, she slammed the door behind her. Going to the phone, she looked up the real estate agency's number and punched it out in quick staccato rhythm. "Mr. Feldman? This is Sheila Danforth. I'm taking my house off the market, at least for the moment. No, I don't care whether someone is interested in it. I've decided not to sell it right now. I'm sorry about the contract I signed with you. Things have changed, and I can't sell the house. Thank you for your understanding. Goodbye." Replacing the receiver in its cradle, Sheila felt all the anger drain from her. In the privacy of her house no one could see her, so she leaned her forehead in her folded arms and wept.

For the next few days Sheila alternated between a flood of tears and anger. She never realized she was capable of such an abundance of either. Not once in all that time did Mike call or come by, and she had no choice but to face the fact that he really might not be back. Marie also noted his absence and asked if she could stay on in Sheila's employ. Sheila was tempted to fire her on the spot, but she was much too depressed to bother with hiring another maid. She gave Marie permission to stay.

A week after the disastrous morning at the beach house, Sheila finally pulled herself together. Mike wasn't coming back, and she had to get on with her life. But the life she'd been living was not what she wanted. Things had to change. She started by calling one of the Danforth Furniture store dealers. Before the day was out, she had sold him all the formal furniture. The next day she had a ladder and several gallons of paint delivered from one of the hardware stores. Within hours the austere white of the dining room had been covered with a friendly pale yellow.

Sheila recalled that as a child she had worked out her frustrations by riding her horse for hours on end. Now she did it with a paintbrush. Before she had stemmed her anger, the living room walls had become a warm cream, the stairwell a pale green and the spare bedroom a Dresden blue. This still didn't bring her peace, so she sewed new curtains for all the upstairs rooms and repapered the shelves in all four baths. By the time she hung the last curtain days later, Sheila was too exhausted to ache for Mike, and she finally slept all night and most of the next morning.

That afternoon she dressed as if she cared how she looked and went shopping for more furniture. The only store she avoided was the Danforth store. She had had more than enough trouble caused by the Danforth Furniture Factory. Instead of the formality favored by George and his expensive designer, Sheila chose furnishings she would be comfortable with. For the first time in her life she was going to be surrounded by her own things. She was assured that everything would be delivered the following week, and she went home tired enough to sleep again that night.

Marie was almost as upset over the sale of all the fine furniture as she had been over Mike's presence. From the look on her face, she must have been thinking that Sheila had lost her mind. But Sheila didn't care. She almost hoped Marie would say something so she would have reason to fire her. All her anger wasn't spent yet.

The following afternoon Gail came over, and Sheila answered the door herself. When Gail stepped in, her mouth dropped open. "Are you remodeling? Where is your furniture?"

"I sold it. Come into the den. I kept most of the things in there."

"But why? And you painted!" Gail sounded as shocked as if Sheila had torn down the back wall of the house.

"I painted most of the large rooms. As for the furniture, I never liked it. I've ordered other things to take its place."

"But—"

"I also took the house off the market. Since I'll be staying here, I decided I wanted the house to reflect me and not George."

"You're staying here?" Gail repeated. "I thought Mike didn't want to live here."

Sheila turned away as if to straighten a picture on the wall. "We've postponed the wedding." She still couldn't believe Mike wouldn't be back. Not when she still felt so much a part of him.

"Perhaps that's best. You were rather rushing into it, you know."

"Would you like some coffee? I'll have Marie bring it in." Sheila left Gail in the den and almost ran down the hall and around the corner. Once in the empty dining room, Sheila leaned back against the sunny wall and closed her eyes. Why hadn't she told Gail the wedding was off? Gail was her best friend. In time everyone would have to know. But not yet. Deep inside, Sheila refused to believe it. If she was wrong—if Mike really did mean all he had said—there would be plenty of time to tell her friends the wedding was off. In the meantime, Sheila planned to stall in the fervent hope that Mike would come to his senses.

Across town, Mike yanked on a bolt deep inside an engine and felt it snap off in his hand. He muttered a curse but refrained from throwing his wrench at the far wall. Only the day before he had broken his clock when one of his screwdrivers had become a projectile. Carl, who was working under a car next to Mike, glanced up with trepidation. Without a word, he slipped back under the car. Mike was trying to figure how he was going to drill out the broken bolt that he couldn't even see. Everything had gone wrong.

Mike straightened and tried to calm down. That day at the beach house he had thought that he could never feel any worse, but he had been wrong. When he had told Sheila goodbye, he had been partially armored with good intentions. Now he wasn't at all sure he had done the right thing, and he was wracked with longing for her.

"If you'll leave it, I'll see what I can do," Carl said helpfully. "I'm smaller, and maybe I can get to it from under the engine."

"I can handle it," Mike snapped, then added a belated, "thanks, anyway." The only thing he could do was to pull the engine out of the car, and that would take several hours and he would make no profit at all on the job. Time was money in this business, and mistakes like this really hurt. It occurred to Mike that he no longer was enjoying any of his work.

"Carl, do you think we could make any money in this town restoring vintage cars?"

"I don't know. I've talked to that man over in Springfield, and he says he has all the business he can handle. But I can't see us doing it in Falls River. Maybe in Mapleton."

Mike shot his younger cousin a suspicious glance. Was he trying to get him to patch things up with Sheila?

"They have a vintage car club over there," Carl added. "There isn't one here."

"I know that."

"I wouldn't mind moving to Mapleton. I've been seeing a girl over there. The town is nice."

Mike made a noncommittal grunt.

"Of course it would cost a bit to get a place set up," Carl continued. "You'd need some special tools to work on the really old ones."

"It's just a dream," Mike said. "I guess it will never come about."

Carl worked in silence for a few minutes, the metallic clanging of his labors echoing in the garage. Finally he slid farther up under the car and said in a muffled voice, "Have you seen Sheila lately?"

"I told you that was all off," Mike growled.

"I know you did, but you're mean as a bear these days. Maybe you ought to go see her."

"Maybe you ought to take care of your own business," Mike growled. He slammed the hood and wiped his hands on his grease rag. "Close up for me. I'm calling it a day."

He went into his office and glanced at the cracked plastic clock on the wall. Closing ten minutes early wouldn't be so bad. He had worked until nearly midnight several days this week—anything to keep from going home to that empty house. He turned the sign on the glass door to read Closed and pulled the door shut behind him.

What really bothered him was the growing suspicion that he was going through all this for nothing. He had gone over his finances, and he made enough money for the monthly payments on that house in Mapleton. Would it really be so bad to use some of Sheila's money for the down payments? If things were different and she had to have a job, he would have no qualms about using her income. But how could he possibly back down now? After that stupid scene he had thrown at the beach house, he wouldn't blame her if she never spoke to him again. What if he went to her and apologized, and she threw him out? That would be more than he could handle. If he was never going to be able to see her again, he could at least hold on to his dignity.

He parked in his driveway but ignored the kids in his neighbor's yard that tried to speak to him. At the moment family scenes were low on his list of enjoyments. The house was cold and dark. He automatically knelt to light the stoves after he switched on the lights. As he glanced up, he noticed that a recent rain had darkened the water spot on the ceiling. Somehow he had to find that hole in the roof and patch it before it got any worse, but at the moment he just couldn't bring himself to do it.

Taking a TV dinner out of the freezer, Mike wrinkled his nose in displeasure. It had looked appetizing in the store, but now the picture on the box looked garish, and he knew the food inside would be as taste-less as everything else had been that week.

He wandered into the bedroom and leaned his arm on the top of his dresser to peer at the photograph of Sheila. He still couldn't bear to put it away, but it haunted him. As for seeing other women, he couldn't bring himself even to consider it. Sheila was the cause of his aching loneliness, and he knew he could never fill her loss with another woman.

From the top drawer of his dresser, Mike took out the blue velvet box that contained Sheila's wedding band. As he opened it, the light sparkled from the facets of gold around the edges. Inside was the in-scription that was so surprisingly identical to the one she had had engraved in his ring. What did one do with an engraved wedding ring when there would be no wedding? Feeling worse than ever, Mike gently closed the box and returned it to the drawer.

As he had done every evening that week, Mike went into the living room and flopped down in front of his television set. He couldn't remember any of the shows he had seen, but at least it had given him something to do. Tonight, if he was really lucky, it might erase Sheila from his mind for a brief respite.

Sheila brushed her hair until her arm ached and her hair gleamed. She pulled a nightgown over her head and stared at her pale reflection in the bathroom mir-ror. She was losing weight, and her skin looked sal-low, as if she had been sick. In a way she felt as if she were. Going to the shoulder-high window, she opened the privacy shutters and peered out at the night.

Somewhere beyond the trees and distant lights was Mike. She had no thoughts that he would be with another woman. She knew he was no more apt to do that than she was to see another man. Not while she could feel their souls still so closely entwined. That meant he was as lonely as she was, and she yearned to comfort him more than she wanted peace for herself.

She rested her folded forearms on the high windowsill and rested her chin upon them. Silently she urged Mike to change his mind and end this fruitless separation.

Chapter Fourteen

Sheila was amazed at how fast word spread that her wedding was postponed. All morning her phone rang with people calling to chat and ask her if it were true. She stuck by her story and maintained enough cool distance to discourage her friends from suggesting that her marriage to Mike Barlow be delayed permanently. Not only would her pride not allow her to admit to others that their relationship might be over, but she couldn't even admit to herself that it might be true. She still clung to hope. She believed in positive thinking, and she believed in Mike Barlow.

The arrival of the furniture van was indeed a welcome sight. Now she had a legitimate reason for not answering the phone. She told Marie to take messages if anyone else called, then answered the front door.

As the burly furniture movers began unloading their cargo, Sheila dashed from room to room trying to stay ahead of the four men to be sure that each piece was placed properly. After everything was in, Sheila took a quick survey to be sure the pieces she had ordered were all there and that nothing would need rearranging. While she had to admit that the formal furniture had been more appropriate for such a grand house, she loved the more casual touch. With a sense of great satisfaction, Sheila signed her acceptance of the delivery and thanked the men for their help.

As the truck was leaving, a car pulled up out front. It was Estelle. Sheila's bubble of happiness was suddenly burst. For a minute she considered having Marie tell Estelle that she wasn't home, but with a deep sigh of resignation she refrained. Eventually she would have to face Estelle, and she felt it was better to get it over with.

When Sheila opened the door, Estelle breezed in without being asked, as was her usual custom. By her smug expression Sheila knew she, too, had heard about the wedding postponement.

"Hello, Sheila. I hope I didn't drop by at an inconvenient time. I see you weren't anticipating company."

Sheila glanced down at her jeans and sweatshirt. "No, I wasn't."

"You never used to go around the house like that. Where on earth did you find those clothes?"

"I see no reason to dress up to move furniture. You must have seen the van as you drove in. Come see what I've done with the house."

"You painted it *green*?" Estelle gasped, staring at the wall behind the stairs.

"Only this room. And it's a celery, not really green." Concealing her smile, Sheila led Estelle to the dining room. "This one is yellow."

"Merciful heaven! It is! And that furniture! Where are all your good things?"

"I sold them. I never did like that stiff, formal look. This is more me." She brushed her fingertips over the polished surface of the oak table. "Come see the living room."

Estelle followed her with obvious trepidation. "You didn't paint it, too, did you?"

"Yes. It's cream. See?"

"Thank goodness. I was afraid it might be yet another color. Sheila, didn't that decorator teach you anything? A house should reflect one major color theme—a neutral one. Not green and yellow."

"And blue. I've been painting upstairs as well."

"Surely you mean you hired it done."

"No, I did it myself."

Estelle walked farther into the room and frowned at the red leather sofa and sling chairs. "Where is your living room suite?"

"I told you I sold it."

"But it was the top of our line! George had it made up especially for this room."

"I got a good price for it, too."

"This looks like a...a dormitory lobby!" As she pointed accusingly at a red director's chair, she said, "You can't expect Nita Rockwell to sit in a chair like that."

"Why would I ask Nita over? She's your friend, not mine."

"Have you forgotten? The committee to draw up the research foundation is meeting here this afternoon."

"I had forgotten all about that."

"Surely you aren't backing out!"

"No, no. I still think a research center would be good for Falls River. I've just had a lot on my mind lately."

"So I see." Estelle touched the red leather cautiously. "I don't recall seeing this design."

"It's not from our factory. I bought it at Tilson-Bach."

Estelle dropped onto the couch and stared at Sheila. "You didn't! Tell me you didn't."

"I did."

"But why on earth would you do that! You know we Danforths all support our family business!"

"I'm also thinking of taking back my maiden name." She paused and waited for Estelle's reaction. She wasn't disappointed.

"You're what? You can't do that! Everyone will think there is some major family split." Estelle was back on her feet.

"I doubt anyone will care much one way or the other. I've always been a bit of an outsider here."

"But an accepted one! If you change your name, it will certainly be remarked upon. Why, I don't even remember what your maiden name was!" At that instant, the implication behind Sheila's suggestion struck Estelle, and her eyes narrowed suspiciously. "If you're still planning to marry Mike Barlow, why would you bother to change your name back?"

Sheila thought fast. The barb about taking her maiden name had been intended to goad Estelle. "A lot of women keep their own name these days. I may hyphenate it. Don't you like the sound of Sheila Atchison-Barlow?"

"No, I don't."

Sheila shrugged. "I haven't decided to do it. It's only an idea."

"Then you really are going ahead with this marriage?"

"Of course," Sheila bluffed. "Had you heard anything to the contrary?"

"Nita said she had heard it might be called off. That's why I came by—to tell you I was glad you had come to your senses."

"Save your congratulations. I still love him."

"Well, all I can say," Estelle commented as she glanced around the room, "is that your tastes have certainly changed since I first met you."

"Yes, they certainly have. I've grown up. I make my own decisions now."

Estelle made no comment, but her lips thinned. "I'll be going." She again looked at the room and shook her head. "Don't forget the meeting here at four."

Sheila gladly closed the door on Estelle and leaned back against it. What would she do if Mike never changed his mind? He was so stubborn, and if she called him first, it might push him farther away. She'd just have to wait, for however long it took.

* * *

Mike had convinced himself that it wasn't fair that he always sent Carl to the parts supplier in Mapleton to pick up his orders, so this time he went himself. And, as he was driving by the Clermont Real Estate Agency, he decided that it wouldn't hurt to stop by and ask for Mrs. Allen.

"Mr. Barlow," she greeted him in her straightforward manner. "Good to see you. Decide on the house?"

"I wanted to talk to you about it. What kind of monthly payment would I be looking at in that house?"

"Depends on your down payment." She tapped figures into her calculator, wrote them down and shoved the paper toward Mike as she leaned back in her swivel desk chair. "These figures on the left are with a minimum down and the others are based on a fairly hefty down payment, as you can see. The less you finance, the smaller your payments will be."

"Yes, I understand that." Mike was mildly perturbed at her inference that he didn't understand the basic principles of financing, but chose to ignore the woman's attitude as he thoughtfully studied the second column. He could afford the monthly payments, but the down payment was clearly beyond his means. He pondered for a moment more, then asked, "Could I see the house again?" He didn't understand why he was doing this, but it seemed important.

"When would you like to go?"

Mike considered changing his mind; it seemed a waste of his time and hers to go see the house again. But he found himself telling her that he wanted to go now, if that was possible. Mrs. Allen quickly agreed and was ushering him out to her car when Mike insisted that he take his own car. When he was through looking, he wanted to be able to leave.

As they walked through the house, Mike managed to set aside the issue of money so he could view the house objectively. The house's lines were gracious, and the floor plan very functional. This was a house that had survived generations of children and could handle many more. As he indulged his fantasies further, he imagined what it would be like if this belonged to him and Sheila and their children. But that just wasn't possible. He didn't have the money for the big down payment. And there were probably other things, too, that would keep this from working out. Fishing for another justification, Mike asked casually, "Have you been in this area long, Mrs. Allen?"

"Most of my life."

"Ever hear of the Danforth family over in Falls River?"

"No, can't say that I have. Here in Mapleton we tend to keep to ourselves. Why do you ask?"

"Oh, nothing. I was just curious." Mike thoughtfully glanced through the downstairs again. If Mrs. Allen was typical of the residents of Mapleton, and Mike felt she must be, then the Barlow-Danforth feud was unknown here and wouldn't pose a problem for him and Sheila. "I'd better have another look at the garage. I'm not sure it will suit my needs."

But as before, he saw the immense detached garage as perfect. Digging further, he asked, "Are there any city restrictions about working on cars here? Not a garage, exactly, but I like to restore old cars. I've thought about making it a business."

"As long as you work back here where you can't be seen from the street, I see no problem. Mapleton doesn't have strict zoning rules. Never needed them. Couldn't put up a sign, of course. Would have to keep the noise down."

"I see." Mike had gotten so caught up in the dream of working on his vintage cars out here that he had forgotten that he was trying to find something other than lack of money to justify not buying the house. He was already planning how he could do his advertising through the local vintage car club and was visualizing one of his own cars entered in their annual exhibition.

"Ready to make an offer?" Mrs. Allen asked hopefully. "I'm sure I could get you in the house right away."

Mike was jolted from his reverie. Everything would work out so well except for the matter of the down payment. Mike tried to hide his disappointment.

"That couple from Manchester is still looking at it," Mrs. Allen confided in the conspiratorial tone of a successful real estate agent who wanted to close the deal. "I'd rather see you have it. They're going through a rival company and, frankly, my commission will be higher if it goes through our own agency." She nodded decisively. "Not trying to rush you. Just wanted you to know. They've seen it twice. They may be drawing up a contract on it right now for all we know. Think about it."

Mike nodded. He wanted this house so badly he could taste it. Not that it was just this particular house, but it had come to represent his life with Sheila. "I'll think about it."

"Don't wait too long. There aren't many houses like this at such a good price."

He nodded and thanked her for showing it to him.

Mike was so preoccupied with his dilemma that he paid for the parts he had come to Mapleton to get, but walked off without them.

As Mike headed back to Falls River, the thought that he could use some of Sheila's money for the down payment plagued him. On the surface it seemed so simple, but Mike couldn't bring himself to accept the idea. He knew Sheila didn't understand the struggle he was going through. How could she? She'd never had to fight for the esteem of others. She might say that her respect for him had nothing to do with money, but she would not continue to respect him if he lost his self-esteem. And this is what would happen if he used her money for the down payment for their home. Somehow he had to figure a way to do this on his own. But right now it looked pretty hopeless.

Estelle strode past Ed's secretary with only a perfunctory wave of her fingers. She had to see him and was in no mood to wait.

Ed was on the phone when she walked in, so she paced his office, impatiently glaring back and forth between Ed and the display of law books that lined one wall of his office. Ed refrained from sighing as he watched her. From long experience he knew that the expression on Estelle's face, coupled with her abrupt movements, meant Estelle was in a vile mood. As soon as he could, he got off the phone and greeted his wife.

"Have you heard? Sheila and Mike have postponed the wedding."

"Oh?"

"Now is our chance. She wouldn't admit it, but I suspect they had a serious argument. Why else would they put it off?"

"And?"

"Don't be so dense, Ed. We have to use this opportunity to break them up for good."

"I assume you have something in mind."

"Go to Barlow and buy his garage."

"I've tried that. He refused in no uncertain terms."

"Offer him more than it's worth. Triple it. Do whatever it takes to get him out of town."

"Are you sure this is worth it? The garage probably does a good business, but it's not a real moneymaker. We wouldn't see a return on our money for quite a while, if at all."

"That's not the point! If we don't come between them now, they may patch up their differences. I just came from the bank and gave them orders to transfer whatever funds you may need from my account."

Ed studied her thoughtfully. Ever since their wedding he and Estelle had maintained separate bank accounts as well as a joint one. She had insisted upon it. This had always been a source of irritation to Ed. For her to offer to use her own money was almost unheard of. "It's that important to you?"

"It's imperative." She glanced at her diamond-encrusted wristwatch. "I have to run. A group of us are meeting at Sheila's house to go over the proposal for the research foundation. Will you get right on it?"

"I'll have my secretary draw up an agreement right away and leave the total amount of the sale blank."

"As a part of the deal, have him agree to leave Falls River and never move back."

"Of course." Ed hated it when Estelle tried to tell him how to do his business.

"Remember, Ed, we have to do whatever it takes. Everyone has a price. Find Barlow's and pay it."

Ed watched her leave and jotted down notes for his secretary to type up. It was rare that Ed got to spend any of Estelle's money, and now she had given him a blank check. Since he was sure that Estelle would take whatever remaining money she had to her grave with her, and he would never see any of it anyway, he had no qualms about doing her bidding. He was looking forward to an interesting afternoon.

Mike was in a foul mood as he unloaded the parts and supplies from his truck. His second trip to Mapleton to pick up his order was bad enough, but on his way back he hadn't been paying attention to his speed and had been stopped by a highway patrolman who had lectured him for nearly twenty minutes before ticketing him and letting him go on his way. A couple of times since he'd gotten back, he had considered closing early and going by Joe's to drown his sorrows, but he knew that would provide him with nothing but a hangover.

As he finished shelving the parts, he noticed a sleek black Lincoln drive up. The car was familiar, but he couldn't place it. Assuming he had a new customer, Mike wiped his hands and headed out front to see what he could do for the man. When he recognized Ed

Simon, Mike's jaw clenched. There was only one reason for him to be there. Stopping in the middle of his work bay, Mike waited for Simon to come to him.

"Hello, Barlow. Nice day."

Mike looked him squarely in the eyes. "Having car trouble, Ed?"

The lawyer frowned at the familiar use of his name, but shook his head and said congenially, "No, I just came out to talk to you. Man to man, so to speak."

Mike bared his teeth in a mock grin. "You sure seem to get a kick out of doing that. I figured the last time you were here was enough."

"Actually, I thought we might talk a little business."

"I told you last time that my garage is not for sale. I thought I'd made that very clear."

"I heard what you said, but we never got around to talking money. What would you take for the garage if you knew money was no object?"

Mike laughed softly. "You want me out of town that bad, do you?"

Ed smiled thinly. "You're very perceptive, Barlow. I do indeed. And I'm willing to work out a reasonable offer for your garage and your assurance in writing that you will move from this town and never return."

"I'm not for sale, either," Mike rumbled as he stepped toward Ed Simon with a threatening scowl.

"Wait a minute, Barlow. You'd better hear me out." Ed tried to hold his ground but had to step back to maintain a distance between them. "Before I came over here, I was talking to a friend of mine over at the courthouse. It's about time for you to renew your towing permit, isn't it?''

Mike stopped, his eyes narrowing to dangerous slits. He was barely able to check his seething anger. "Next week, I believe. You wouldn't be threatening to block my renewal, would you?"

"No, no." Ed held his hands up and shook his head as if he would never take part in such shady dealings. "Why, without a towing permit, you wouldn't do very well operating a garage like this. Would you?" The smile was back on his lips, but his eyes were steely.

Grimly Mike looked around at the old building, then back to Ed Simon, but he didn't speak. He was trying to calm himself and collect his thoughts. As his anger began to subside, his reasoning returned. He wasn't sure whether Ed's friend could keep him from renewing his towing permit, but odds were that he might. Money spoke very loudly, and in those terms, he didn't have much of a voice.

Then it came to Mike that if he was very clever, he might be able to turn the tables on Mr. Edward Simon, attorney-at-law.

Without changing expressions, Mike began, "This garage has been in my family for generations. You understand all about family pride, don't you?"

"I was thinking of offering, say, one hundred thousand."

"I have more family pride than that," Mike countered. It was a gamble. If he pushed Ed too hard, and Ed did have a way to block his permit, Mike stood a chance of losing everything. Mike waited patiently for Ed's next move.

After a long pause, Ed Simon decided to sweeten the offer. "If we do reach agreement, you won't have any use for your house here. I believe you live on Andrews Street?"

"You're more thorough than I expected. So what?"

"I'm also prepared to buy your house."

"Are you now?" If Ed Simon had intended to play his trump card, he wouldn't have taken this tack. The permit thing was a bluff. Mike was beginning to enjoy this. "Just what did you have in mind?"

"The houses in that neighborhood go for, oh, say forty-five thousand."

"Not that particular house. I've become very attached to it."

"I think that's a fair price, but I might be able to do a little better than that."

"You mentioned you wanted my plans to leave town in writing. I'm assuming you would want me to sign some kind of document?"

"As a matter of fact," Ed said as he reached into his coat pocket, "I happen to have just such a paper right here."

"My signature is awfully expensive," Mike replied. "You understand, of course."

"Certainly." Ed paused as he considered just what it would take to buy this man out. He was tired of playing the game, and besides, it was Estelle's money, not his. He named a sum that caused Mike to glance at him in surprise. "That's for the garage, the house, and your signature."

Mike barely managed to keep from laughing out loud. He wouldn't need Sheila's money for the down payment. He could buy the house outright and still have money left over. "I would have to keep my truck, my tools, and my portable equipment. After all, that's how I make my living."

Ed smiled frostily. "As long as you don't make your living here in Falls River, I don't care if you gut the place."

"That's a deal." Mike took the paper and pulled a pen from his shirt pocket. After his name was written across the bottom of the agreement, he said, "I have to admit, I'd have settled for less. You tossed this money away as if it wasn't even your own."

Ed took the paper and folded it carefully. "It wasn't. Good day, Mr. Barlow. And goodbye."

Mike shrugged. He couldn't care less if the Danforths had taken up a door-to-door campaign as long as he had the money. When Ed drove off, Mike opened the door to the office where Carl was working on the monthly billing. "Carl, how would you like to move to Mapleton?"

"You mean it?"

"Ed Simon just bought me out. Mark all those bills 'Paid in Full' and put the Closed sign on the door. We're in the vintage car restoration business now." He closed the door on Carl's joyous whoop.

Mike drove first to the Simons' bank and asked that the check be reissued to him as a cashier's check, so his bank would immediately honor one of such a large amount. Then he deposited it in his own bank. Next he called Mrs. Allen in Mapleton and made her a cash offer of ten thousand dollars less than the asking price for the house. Ten minutes later she called Mike back, verifying that the offer would be accepted and that she would immediately draw up the contract. Laughing from sheer happiness, he started toward Sheila's house.

Sheila was trying hard to concentrate on what Estelle was saying, but her heart really wasn't in it. Mike still hadn't called, and her fears that he might never do so were mounting. She had debated all afternoon about calling him, but had postponed it each time. She had her pride, too, but more importantly, she was desperately afraid that he would reject her.

The women that Estelle had invited to Sheila's house for their meeting all sat in the living room, looking around them with a great deal of curiosity. On top of the rumors that Sheila's wedding was called off, they were obviously wondering about her new decorating scheme. Although Sheila knew from experience that they were whispering among themselves when she was out of earshot, no one said a word to her. Even their usual gratuitous compliments were markedly absent. But Sheila didn't care that they disapproved. She hadn't made the changes for them; she had done it for herself. Gail asked a question about the foundation's purpose, and Sheila tried to follow Estelle's answer, but her mind kept wandering back to Mike.

Each time she thought of him, her sadness grew. When she felt she could take no more, something in her mind clicked, and she realized that she couldn't just sit idly by and lose the only thing that had ever been important to her. The time when Sheila would have passively accepted her fate was gone. Screwing up her courage to face his possible rejection, Sheila decided that when this meeting was over, she would go see Mike and somehow convince him that material things were not important to her.

The ringing of the doorbell brought Sheila's attention back into focus. After Estelle looked around the room, she asked, "Isn't everyone already here? Who could that be?"

"I'll go see." Sheila waved Marie back and opened the door. Mike was standing on her doorstep, and he had never looked so good. He wore the tight jeans that she so admired on him, and his shirt was tapered close to his sides. He, too, had lost some weight during their separation, but his rugged appeal had only been strengthened. The sunlight glowed in his blond hair, and although the corners of his mouth were barely upturned in the hint of a grin, Sheila could see laughter in his eyes.

For a moment they quietly stared at each other. Then Mike said, "Will you marry me?"

Sheila bit back her tears of joy. "When?"

"Right now. Today. I have your ring with me."

"Yes," she whispered. "I will."

Estelle's voice called from the other room, "Who's at the door?"

"Come with me now," Mike urged. "Right now."

"Can I get your ring first?"

"Will it take you long?"

Sheila kissed him lightly before running for the stairs. She hurried to her room and grabbed her purse as well as his ring. Should she take any clothes? She didn't know if he meant to leave town or merely the house. He had said he wanted her to hurry. No, she decided, if they were going away she could buy whatever she needed when she got wherever they were going.

Brushing the tears of happiness from the corners of her eyes, she rushed back downstairs, paused for a second to compose herself, then poked her head into the living room. Interrupting the conversation, she said, "I agree to support the foundation, Estelle, and I agree with the ground rules you've set up, except for one detail—I'm going to be the director. Don't look so shocked. You can be on the board. I'll start the fund with a sizable donation, but the rest will have to come from fund-raising."

"But—"

"I'd love to stay and discuss this with you, but I really must go."

"Where! Where are you going!" Estelle demanded, rising from her chair.

"To be married!" Sheila called back as she ran out the door and into Mike's embrace.

As he held her tightly to him and kissed her, the warmth of his love spread from her lips throughout her body. At length, he pulled back. "You're sure?" he asked softly.

"I've never been more certain of anything in my life."

"Then let's go."

"Where are we going?" she asked as she hurried with him to his car.

He grinned. "I'm taking you home."

COMING NEXT MONTH

VOYAGE OF THE NIGHTINGALE—Billie Green
Braving exotic poisons and native sacrifices, cultured Bostonian
Rachel McNaught scoured the tropics for her missing brother. But
what she found was ruffian sailor Flynn, who scorned her money...and
stole her heart.

SHADOW OF DOUBT—Caitlin Cross
Who *was* widow Julia Velasco? A decadent gold digger who'd kidnapped
her own son for profit? Or a desperate mother in need of protection?
Mesmerized by her, attorney Anson Wolfe sought the elusive truth.

THE STAR SEEKER—Maggi Charles
"Your lover will be tall, dark and handsome," the palm-reader told
her. But shopkeeper Hilary Forsythe was avoiding men—particularly
banker J.A. Mahoney, who handled her business loan...and mismanaged
her emotions!

IN THE NAME OF LOVE—Paula Hamilton
Madcap Samantha Graham was determined to join the CIA. Agent
Jim Collins was bedazzled but skeptical. To "protect" her from her
impulsive self, would he ruin her chances—in the name of love?

COME PRIDE, COME PASSION—Jennifer West
When Cade Delaney returned to Dixie, he had bitter revenge on his
mind. The object: proud Elizabeth Hart. The obstacle: his burning
passion for her.

A TIME TO KEEP—Curtiss Ann Matlock
Jason Kenyon was old enough to be Lauren Howard's father, but that
didn't stop them from falling in love. Could their precious time together
last...or would the odds against them tear them apart?

AVAILABLE THIS MONTH:

CRISTEN'S CHOICE
Ginna Gray

PURPLE DIAMONDS
Jo Ann Algermissen

WITH THIS RING
Pat Warren

RENEGADE SON
Lisa Jackson

A MEASURE OF LOVE
Lindsay McKenna

HIGH SOCIETY
Lynda Trent

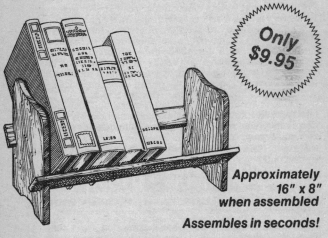

If you're ready for a more sensual, more provocative reading experience...

We'll send you 4 Silhouette Desire novels FREE and without obligation

Then, we'll send you six more Silhouette Desire® novels to preview every month for 15 days with absolutely no obligation! When you decide to keep them, you pay just $1.95 each ($2.25 each in Canada) *with never any additional charges!*

And that's not all. You get FREE home delivery of all books as soon as they are published and a FREE subscription to the Silhouette Books Newsletter as long as you remain a member. Each issue is filled with news on upcoming titles, interviews with your favorite authors, even their favorite recipes.

Silhouette Desire novels are not for everyone. They are written especially for the woman who wants a more satisfying, more deeply involving reading experience. Silhouette Desire novels take you *beyond* the others.

If you're ready for that kind of experience, fill out and return the coupon today!

Silhouette ❤ Desire®

Silhouette Books, 120 Brighton Rd., P.O. Box 5084, Clifton, NJ 07015-5084

FOUR UNIQUE SERIES
FOR EVERY WOMAN YOU ARE...

Silhouette Romance

Heartwarming romances that will make you
laugh and cry as they bring you all the wonder
and magic of falling in love.

*6 titles
per month*

Silhouette Special Edition

Expanded romances written with emotion and
heightened romantic tension to ensure
powerful stories. A rare blend of passion and
dramatic realism.

*6 titles
per month*

Silhouette Desire

Believable, sensuous, compelling—and
above all, romantic—these stories deliver
the promise of love, the guarantee
of satisfaction.

*6 titles
per month*

Silhouette Intimate Moments

Love stories that entice; longer, more
sensuous romances filled with adventure,
suspense, glamour and melodrama.

*4 titles
per month*

Silhouette Romances
not available in retail outlets in Canada

SIL-GEN-1A